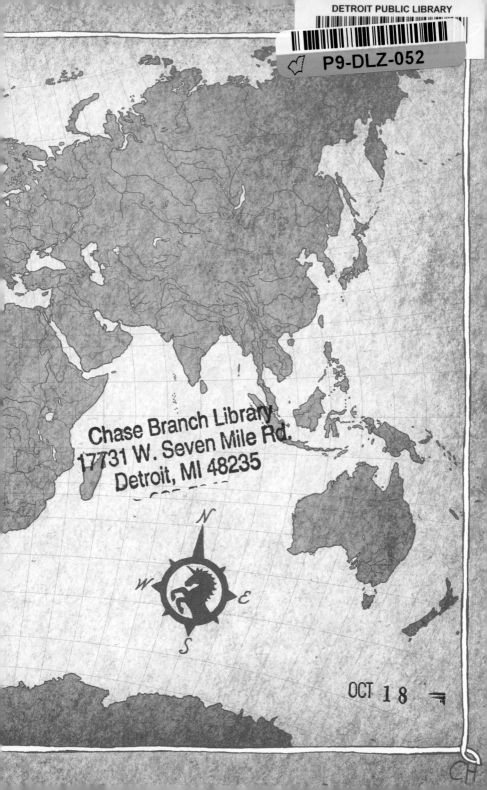

THE UNICORN RESCUE SOCIETY

THE BASQUE DRAGON

ALSO BY
ADAM GIDWITZ:

A Tale Dark and Grimm

In a Glass Grimmly

The Grimm Conclusion

*The Inquisitor's Tale:
Or The Three Magical Children
and Their Holy Dog*

*The Unicorn Rescue Society:
The Creature of the Pines*

THE UNICORN RESCUE SOCIETY

THE BASQUE DRAGON

BY Adam Gidwitz & Jesse Casey

ILLUSTRATED BY Hatem Aly

CREATED BY Jesse Casey, Adam Gidwitz,
and Chris Lenox Smith

DUTTON CHILDREN'S BOOKS

DUTTON CHILDREN'S BOOKS

Penguin Young Readers Group
An imprint of Penguin Random House LLC
375 Hudson Street
New York, NY 10014

Library of Congress Cataloging-in-Publication Data
Names: Gidwitz, Adam, author. | Casey, Jesse, author. | Aly, Hatem, illustrator.
Title: The Basque dragon / by Adam Gidwitz & Jesse Casey ; illustrated by Hatem Aly.
Description: New York, NY : Dutton Children's Books, [2018] | Series: The Unicorn Rescue
Society ; 2 | Summary: "Elliot and Uchenna join Professor Fauna on another adventure—
a trip to the Basque country where they have to save a herensuge from the billionaire
Schmoke Brothers"—Provided by publisher. | Identifiers: LCCN 2018001395 |
ISBN 9780735231733 (hardback) | ISBN 9780735231740 (epub) | Subjects: | CYAC:
Animals, Mythical—Fiction. | Animal rescue—Fiction. | Dragons—Fiction. | Friendship—
Fiction. | Paâis Vasco (Spain)—Fiction. | BISAC: JUVENILE FICTION / Legends, Myths,
Fables / General. | JUVENILE FICTION / Social Issues / Friendship. | JUVENILE
FICTION / Historical / General. | Classification: LCC PZ7.G3588 Bas 2018 |
DDC [Fic]—dc23 | LC record available at https://lccn.loc.gov/2018001395

Printed in the United States of America
1   3   5   7   9   10   8   6   4   2

Edited by Julie Strauss-Gabel
Design by Anna Booth
Text set in Legacy Serif ITC Std

To Zachary: you're the Uchenna to my Elliot...
(either that, or my personal Professor Fauna)
—A.G.

To Sarah
—J.C.

To my wife, Michelle, who crossed the ocean
back and forth for us to be together
—H.A.

UNICORNS ARE REAL.

At least, I think they are.

Dragons are definitely real. I have seen them. Chupacabras exist, too. Also Sasquatch. And mermaids—though they are *not* what you think.

But back to unicorns. When I, Professor Mito Fauna, was a young man, I lived in the foothills of Peru. One day, there were rumors in my town of a unicorn in danger, far up in the mountains. At that instant I founded the Unicorn Rescue Society—I was the only member—and set off to save the unicorn. When I finally located it, though, I saw that it was *not* a unicorn, but rather a qarqacha, the legendary two-headed llama of the Andes. I was very slightly disappointed. I rescued it anyway. Of course.

Now, many years later, there are members of the Unicorn Rescue Society all around the world. We are sworn to protect all the creatures of myth and legend. Including unicorns! If we ever find them! Which I'm sure we will!

But our enemies are powerful and ruthless, and we are in desperate need of help. Help from someone brave and kind and curious, and brave. (Yes, I said "brave" twice. It's important.)

Will you help us? Will you risk your very *life* to protect the world's mythical creatures?

Will you join the Unicorn Rescue Society?

I hope so. The creatures need you.

Defende Fabulosa! Protege Mythica!

Mito Fauna, DVM, PhD, EdD, etc.

CHAPTER ONE

Elliot Eisner was lying, facedown, on the pavement in front of his new house, in his new town, in New Jersey.

The morning was clear and fine. Kids were walking past on their way to school, kicking red and yellow leaves. It smelled of fall.

Why was Elliot lying facedown on the pavement?

He wasn't sure. He had opened his front door, stepped on something, and then gone

toppling headfirst down the steps. Elliot pushed
himself up and turned around to see what he
had tripped on.

On his front step was a small package,
wrapped in brown paper. He got to his feet and
walked over to the package. No address. No
stamps. Just a name, scrawled in brown ink.
Weird. He examined the name on the package.

It was his name.

Elliot had had a *strange* day yesterday. It had been his first day at his new school. He'd made a friend, Uchenna Devereaux. She was odd. She kinda dressed like a punk rocker, she made up random songs about nothing at all, and she had a strong desire to put herself, and Elliot, in mortal danger. All that said, she was funny and she was brave and Elliot liked her. They had rescued a young Jersey Devil—which was supposed to be an imaginary creature, but definitely was *not* imaginary. It seemed to have adopted them. Finally, a terrifying teacher at their school, named Professor Fauna, had invited them to join a secret organization: the Unicorn Rescue Society. Its mission was to save mythical creatures from danger.

So yeah, it had been a strange day.

Now Elliot was staring at a mysterious package that had been left on his doorstep.

For him.

He tore open the paper. A book stared up at him. *The Country of Basque.*

"What?" Elliot said out loud, to no one.

Why had someone left him a book? On his doorstep? And who had left it? And couldn't he just have a normal, not-at-all dangerous second day at South Pines Elementary? Please?

He sighed, tucked the book under his arm, threw his backpack over his shoulder, and started off to school.

CHAPTER TWO

Uchenna Devereaux normally left her house with one shoe untied, half her homework still under the bed upstairs, playing air guitar, and singing a song she'd made up that morning in the shower.

But not today.

She opened her front door and looked down her street in both directions before slipping out into the cool autumn morning. She put her backpack over her shoulders, pulled the straps tight, and began walking, warily, to school. Yesterday had been a weird day.

She had made a new friend named Elliot. He wasn't exactly *cool*—he got nervous easily, he memorized entire books about things that could kill him, and he was definitely *not* rock-and-roll. But he was smart and funny, and Uchenna liked him. Also, they'd met a Jersey Devil and been invited by the school's weirdest teacher to join a secret society. This secret society had very rich and very powerful enemies: the Schmoke brothers, two billionaires who owned businesses all over the world, and half their little town.

Also, Uchenna and Elliot and that weird teacher *may* have broken into the Schmoke brothers' mansion.

Okay, they definitely did.

Which was why Uchenna was being so vigilant this morning on her walk to school. As she turned the corner from her block onto the main street, she glanced over her shoulder. A few blocks away lay the wealthiest neighborhood in town—where the Schmoke brothers' mansion was. Beyond that, in the distance, she could just make out the towering smokestacks of the Schmoke Industries power plant, billowing black plumes into the air. She—*FTHUMP!*

Uchenna sat down hard on her rear end. A small, thin boy with curly brown hair was lying on his back on the sidewalk, staring up into space. An open book lay on the sidewalk behind him.

"Elliot!" Uchenna exclaimed.

"Ow," said Elliot.

"I didn't see you there!"

"That's good. The alternative would have been that you *did* see me there and ambushed me on purpose."

Uchenna laughed and got to her feet. "Come on. Let's get to school."

Elliot lay unmoving on the ground. "I don't think so. Today's been pretty messed up already. School's only going to make it worse."

Uchenna grabbed Elliot by the wrist and pulled him to his feet. She scooped up *The Country of Basque* and handed it to him. "Let's go. However messed up today's going to be, it'll be better if we face it together."

As Elliot brushed off his khaki pants, he squinted at Uchenna. "Your positivity disgusts me."

Uchenna grinned, threw her arm around Elliot's shoulders, and dragged him toward school.

CHAPTER THREE

Elliot and Uchenna sat at the far end of one of the long tables in the school cafeteria, waiting for the morning bell to ring. Kids were streaming in the double doors, finding their friends, laughing, clowning, discussing whatever they'd seen on television or online the night before.

Not Elliot and Uchenna, though. Elliot was telling Uchenna about the mysterious book on his doorstep. "I haven't read much of it yet. Just the first five chapters."

"You read the first five chapters between your house and the corner where we knocked into each other? That's one block!"

"They're short chapters. And I read pretty fast."

"So, what did you learn?"

"Well, I learned about the Basque people, the Euskaldunak."

"The AY-oo-SKAL-doo-nak?"

"Yeah. They're kinda amazing. They're these fierce mountain people, who've lived nestled between Spain and France and the sea, for thousands of years. Pretty much every great empire of Europe has tried to conquer them, but no one could."

"They sound awesome."

"Definitely."

"Any idea *why* you're reading this book? Or who gave it to you?"

"I have two guesses. Both frighten me."

Uchenna shrugged. "You *are* easily frightened."

"One possibility is the Schmoke brothers."

"Okay," Uchenna said, "that would frighten me, too. But why would the Schmoke brothers leave you a *book*?"

"No idea. A warning? The other person who could have left it for me is—"

At that very moment, the cafeteria doors crashed open, and in strode a tall, wiry man with a black-and-white beard and a shock of hair exploding from his skull. He wore an old tweed suit and shoes that had probably been expensive forty years ago. From under his shaggy eyebrows, his eyes roved the faces of the nearby students—who cowered before him.

Which was not surprising, because he looked like he might attack someone.

The man's name was Professor Mito Fauna.

"The other possibility," Elliot continued, subtly gesturing at the man, who was now peering around the cafeteria as if he were looking for his next victim, "is him."

CHAPTER FOUR

Professor Fauna's eyes landed on Uchenna and Elliot, like a predator finding its prey. He began to weave in and out of the lunch tables, making his way toward them. He moved with a crackling, manic energy that made everyone—teachers and kids alike—jump out of his way.

He arrived at their table, glancing at the other kids nearby and then running his big brown hands through his wiry hair, making it stand up even straighter.

"*Buenos días, mis amigos*," Professor Fauna said. He was from Peru, and his voice was rich and rocky and slightly accented. He could easily have played a secret agent in an action movie—if the secret agent had been lost in the wilderness for ten years without a change of clothes or a comb. "I hope you have recovered from our adventures of yesterday."

Every kid at the table turned to stare, first at the professor, and then at Elliot and Uchenna.

"Uh, hi, Professor," said Elliot.

"Yup," added Uchenna quickly. "Doing fine."

Professor Fauna nodded. Then, he hesitated. He began shifting awkwardly from foot to foot. Clearly, he wanted to say something to Uchenna and Elliot, but felt he could not with all the other kids around. He noticed the book that Elliot had been reading. "Ah!" he said. "You received my package! I am glad it did not fall into the wrong hands!"

Professor Fauna suddenly seemed to realize

how strange that sounded. He looked around. Absolutely every kid within earshot was staring at him. He cleared his throat. "Uh, for example, the, uh, the hands of a clock! Those would be . . . wrong . . . because clocks . . . cannot read!"

"What?" both Elliot and Uchenna said at once.

"Never mind!" said the professor quickly. "Anyway, I would like to request your attendance after school for a meeting of the, um, *club* we spoke of yesterday."

One of the kids at the table, a freckly boy named Lucas, asked, "What club, Mr. Fauna? Can I join, too?"

"It is the, uh, club for . . . ," Professor Fauna stammered. "For the history, uh, and the philosophy of . . ."

Elliot and Uchenna could see that the professor was struggling to come up with a believable cover story. They both tried to think of the worst, most terrible idea for a club they could, so that none of the other kids would want to come. Unfortunately, they blurted out their ideas at the same time.

"Nutrition," said Uchenna.

"Worms," said Elliot.

"What?" said Lucas.

"Yes, the Worm-Nutrition Club!" exclaimed Professor Fauna, thrusting a long finger into the air. "We will be discussing how to feed and care for worms."

Some of the kids at the table snickered.

"Mostly, we find that they like poop," the professor added.

"Ugh!" someone groaned.

"Chicken poop, they like. And duck poop, too. Cat poop, on the other hand—"

"They get the idea, Professor," said Uchenna.

Lucas looked positively queasy. "Actually, I have soccer after school."

Professor Fauna beamed at Elliot and Uchenna and then winked. They rolled their eyes. "Come to my office. You know where it is." He gave them a little salute and then strode away through the cafeteria.

A girl leaned toward Uchenna. "You've seen his office? I heard he has a torture chamber under the school. Is that true?"

Uchenna looked at Elliot. He shrugged.

"Something like that," Uchenna replied.

CHAPTER FIVE

Uchenna and Elliot stood at the top of a dark stairwell. The bell had rung, and kids were rushing outside to take advantage of the beautiful fall day. They would be playing kickball or tag or lounging under a maple tree with bright red leaves. Whereas Uchenna and Elliot were gazing down a narrow staircase to the basement, where they'd find another stairway to the sub-basement, where they'd find a small door that led to Professor Fauna's office.

"Are you sure you want to do this?" Uchenna asked.

"Absolutely not," said Elliot.

"Do your mom and grandma know you're here?"

"I called and told them I was joining the band."

"Oh! Cool," said Uchenna. "What instrument do you play?"

"None. I'm not really joining the band. I'm here with you."

"Right."

"Did you tell your parents?"

"Yeah," said Uchenna. "I called and told them I was joining the basketball team."

"Oh! Cool. What position do you play?"

"What? I don't. I'm—"

Elliot interrupted her. "I was kidding."

"Oh."

Silence fell. The kids gazed down the long, dark stairwell again.

"Well?" said Uchenna at last. "Wanna go hang out with some weird dude in a basement?"

"Not really. But I guess it'll be better if we face it together."

Uchenna threw her arm around his shoulders. "See? That's what I'm talking about."

Elliot sighed.

They descended the stairs, found the second staircase, and descended that one, too. They walked along a dark and narrow hallway with a filthy, rough cement floor. Uchenna began to sing a song with very little melody.

"Elliot and Uchenna
walking in the spooky basement.
Hopefully, no weirdos
jump out from the dark and kill them."

Elliot shuddered. "Can't you make up something happier?"

"That was in the style of Lou Reed. He said to write about real life," Uchenna replied. But she decided to hum the rest of the song instead of inventing more lyrics.

Finally, they came to a door with a sign that said: JANITORIAL SUPPLIES. Except someone had partially covered it with a handwritten nameplate that read:

Uchenna knocked. Instantly, they heard the sound of dead bolts being thrown—*click, clack,*

clunk, kerchunk, kerplunk. Five heavy-duty locks. For the social studies department? The door slowly swung open, revealing the tall man with the tattered suit and the threatening eyes.

"Children! *¡Fantástico!*" exclaimed the professor, as if he were surprised it was them and not some mortal enemy of his. "Please come in. We have much to discuss."

They entered a room that wasn't much bigger than the inside of a large car. Three walls were lined with floor-to-ceiling shelves that bent under the weight of an enormous collection of books. At first glance, the fourth wall appeared to be covered with the world's weirdest wallpaper. But it wasn't wallpaper—it was charts and maps, thumbtacked on top of one another in a crazy patchwork and crammed with handwritten notes and drawings. Against that wall a cramped desk piled high with notebooks, tabloid newspapers, and fast-food-meal toys. The place looked like it had been hit by a hurricane and then a tornado and then a pack of rabid raccoons. Even so, the children got the sense that it was governed by some strange organizational system known only to the professor.

Professor Fauna closed the door behind them and locked the five dead bolts. The sound of each one made Elliot wince. "Thank you both for coming. As new members of the Unicorn Rescue Society, I will be training you to—"

Just then, a blur of blue and red shot out from behind the only chair and collided with Elliot's head. Elliot screamed and tumbled backward.

He writhed against a wall of books, his face being attacked by a strange creature with soft blue fur and bright red wings.

"It's only Jersey!" Uchenna said. The young Jersey Devil was now clinging to Elliot's face, his tiny claws hooked on to Elliot's skin.

"Ow! Ow! Get it off!" Elliot cried.

"I think he missed you," Uchenna observed.

"I appreciate the sentiment, but he's still digging his *talons* into my *face*!"

Uchenna took the Jersey Devil under his forelegs and moved him to her lap. She stroked the thick fur that covered his bony head. He began to purr.

"Fascinating," the professor said. "All day he has been sleeping under that chair. Never could I rouse him. I thought perhaps he had some laziness disorder."

The Jersey Devil raised his head and growled at the professor.

"But perhaps he just missed you! Anywhat, I have received a message from a member of the Unicorn Rescue Society. I need your help."

Uchenna sat up in her chair. Jersey sat up in Uchenna's lap. But Elliot crossed his arms, narrowed his eyes, and said, "Professor, we're not going to help you until you answer some questions. Uchenna and I feel very uncomfortable hanging out with a teacher in the basement after school, and not telling our parents about it. Not to mention breaking into the Schmoke brothers' home! Speaking of which, tell us how you know them in the first pl—"

"NO!" Professor Fauna shouted.

Elliot and Uchenna stepped back, stunned.

The professor cleared his throat. "I mean . . . *not now*. Time is of the essence! A herensuge is missing!"

"A *what*?"

"A HAIR-en-SOO-gai! The dragon of the Basque Country!"

Uchenna and Elliot were momentarily stupefied. Finally, Uchenna stammered, "Isn't the Basque Country in *Europe*?"

"Right! That's why we have no time to lose!"

Elliot said, "You want us to go to Europe *now*?"

"Of course!"

"To rescue a *dragon*?"

"*¡Mala palabra!* Why are you suddenly so stupid? It is like your brains are moving through jars of honey! Yes! We must go to Europe, to rescue a dragon, now!"

The kids spoke at exactly the same time.

Elliot said, "Absolutely not."

And Uchenna said, "Awesome."

CHAPTER SIX

"This morning," the professor told them, as he hurried through the corridors of the school's sub-basement, Elliot and Uchenna straining to keep up, with Jersey's head poking out of Uchenna's backpack, "I was contacted by an old friend. His name is Mitxel Mendizabal." It sounded like MEE-chel men-DIZ-uh-bahl. "Mitxel is a member of the Unicorn Rescue Society living in Bizkaia, in the Basque Country."

"Bizkaia," said Elliot. "That's where the

Basque people won the freedom to live under the *foruak*, their traditional laws, from the king of Spain."

The professor missed a step, and half turning to Elliot, said, "You have already made much progress in the book I gave you!"

"Yeah, but why did you leave it on my doorstep? And how did you know where I live?" Elliot asked.

Professor Fauna waved his hand dismissively. "It doesn't matter."

"It matters to me," Elliot objected.

But Uchenna was suddenly feeling cheated. "Why did you give Elliot the book, and not me?"

The professor said, "Do you make a habit of memorizing entire books in a single day?"

"No, but—"

"Besides, I have something else for you. It is in my airplane. Now, *vámonos!*"

"You have a *plane*?" Elliot practically shouted as the professor climbed a small staircase to a door marked EMERGENCY EXIT ONLY. DO NOT OPEN. ALARM WILL SOUND.

"Of course! I keep it in the faculty parking lot for just such occasions." He pushed the door open. No alarm went off.

They emerged into the bright light of the fall afternoon. The parking lot was crowded with the cars of teachers and custodians, lunch ladies and secretaries.

And then they spotted it. Occupying the three

parking spaces between Principal Kowalski's seafoam green hatchback and Miss Vole's motorcycle was an airplane. It wasn't a big plane—it had a single propeller on its nose and a cabin that looked about half the size of Professor Fauna's office. The top of the plane was pale blue, and its underbelly was white, and both top and bottom were scarred with years of rust and dents.

The professor unlocked the plane's door, then boosted Elliot and Uchenna up into the cockpit, pulling himself in behind them.

"Buckle up, children," he warned. "The take-off can be somewhat bumpy."

"This plane can fly across the *Atlantic Ocean*?" Uchenna asked.

"Of course! She is very reliable. I call her the *Phoenix*. As you may know, the phoenix is a mythical creature that dies in a burst of fire and then rises again from its own ashes. This plane is very much like that. Many times has it crashed. But always I can get it working again!"

"I don't want to do this," Elliot said. "I don't want to do this. I don't want to do this."

But Professor Fauna had already started up the plane. He locked the doors.

"Buckle up!" the professor cried over the roar of the propeller. Elliot and Uchenna grabbed the seat belts. Jersey scampered from Uchenna's bag onto her lap. She gripped him to her chest.

The plane lurched forward. Elliot dug his fingers into the armrests of his seat. Professor

Fauna guided the plane to the driveway of the faculty parking lot. He began to pick up speed. Faster and faster they went, the little *Phoenix* rumbling on its three wheels. They were rapidly approaching the end of the driveway, which led out onto a busy street.

"Good gracious, good gracious, good gracious," Elliot whimpered. Uchenna grabbed his hand.

Just before reaching the intersection, the professor yanked back on the control stick. The plane's nose rose, and the *Phoenix* shot up in the air, narrowly avoiding the traffic whizzing by below. The force of the lift-off pressed them all against the backs of their seats, and pushed Jersey flat against Uchenna. They were climbing.

Suddenly, Elliot realized he had been screaming. He closed his mouth. Uchenna was also making a great deal of noise. But she wasn't screaming. She was whooping.

"THIS IS AMAZING!" she shouted.

The plane banked, and they could see the school, the trees, their houses, and even the smokestacks of the Schmoke Industries factory far below.

"WOOO-HOOOO!" Uchenna cried.

Elliot put his head between his knees.

CHAPTER SEVEN

"Professor!" Elliot said, his head resting against the small window beside him, his face positively green as he stared out at the blue sky and, below them, the clouds. "My mom expects me home for dinner. A flight to Europe must take hours and hours! Then we'll have to fly back. And, oh yeah, *rescue a dragon* while we're there."

"Don't worry, Elliot. The Basque Country is

in a different time zone. We can go and be back in time for dinner."

"That's not how time zones work, Professor."

"I'm pretty sure it is."

Uchenna nodded. "I think he's right, Elliot."

Suddenly, the plane lurched in a gust of wind. Elliot closed his eyes and tried not to be sick.

Uchenna turned to the professor. "So, you said you have something for me?"

"Oh yes!" He turned away from the steering column and began digging behind his seat. With no one manning the controls, the plane took a sudden jag downward. Elliot screamed. Jersey was thrown into the air. Uchenna grabbed the steering yoke and pulled up. The plane leveled out. Professor Fauna reemerged as if nothing had happened, holding a camouflage backpack.

"What's that?" Uchenna asked.

"It is a special Jersey Devil transporter!"

"Where *is* Jersey, by the way?" Elliot asked.

They looked up. Jersey was clinging to the ceiling, his little legs trembling.

"He must not be used to flying!" the professor said.

"He has wings, Professor," Elliot replied. "I think he's just not used to flying in a custommade death trap."

Uchenna was examining the backpack. Tiny holes had been poked in the main compartment, and the two side compartments had been insulated.

"Those are for his food," the professor explained. "I made it last night."

"You *made* this?" Uchenna said. She was impressed.

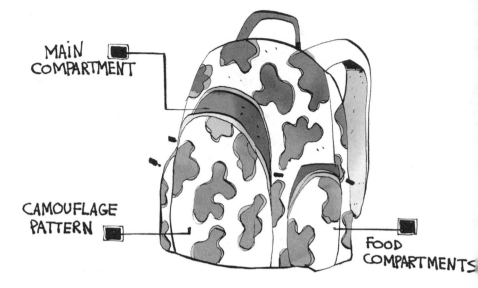

MAIN
COMPARTMENT

CAMOUFLAGE
PATTERN

FOOD
COMPARTMENTS

Jersey dropped down into Elliot's lap. Elliot gazed out of the window. They were *flying*. To *the Basque Country*. In *Europe*. His mom and grandma were going to *kill* him.

Elliot remembered that the professor hadn't answered any of his questions before whisking them off to his frequently-crashes-but-always-works-again-somehow airplane. "Professor, can we talk about the Schmoke brothers now?"

The plane jerked downward, and everyone was thrust forward against their seat belts.

"Sorry!" said the professor. "Turbulence."

Elliot was pretty sure that Professor Fauna had made the plane do that intentionally. It was highly suspicious. He was about to ask about the Schmoke brothers again when Uchenna asked her own question:

"When you say we're supposed to rescue a *dragon,* what exactly do you mean?" Uchenna asked. "Like a giant fire-breathing lizard that sleeps on a huge pile of treasure? Because I definitely want to see one of those."

Professor Fauna sighed as he squinted at the endless stretch of blue before them. "Uchenna, do not be swayed by the video films you see on the television. Dragons are not all giant fire-breathers. Some are quite small. Some swim underwater. Some have cool, refreshing, frosty breath. Think about birds: There are eagles, there are chickens, and there are ostriches. All are very different, but all are birds. It is the same with dragons."

"So, what kind of dragon is a herensuge?" Uchenna said.

"Well, in this specific case, you were correct," the professor admitted. "The herensuge is exactly what you described."

Elliot groaned and began petting Jersey rather hard. He wasn't sure whether he was trying to comfort the little Jersey Devil, or himself.

Uchenna tapped Professor Fauna on his tweed-covered shoulder. "Can I try flying the plane?"

"NO!" Elliot shouted.

The professor smiled. "Perhaps another time."

CHAPTER EIGHT

Uchenna stared out the plane's front window. They'd been flying for what seemed like *forever*, and most of the flight had been over clouds and flat blue ocean.

Elliot had put Jersey into the new backpack, where the little creature had promptly turned invisible and fallen asleep. Elliot then opened *The Country of Basque*. He kept finding interesting information in it that he would relay to Uchenna and the professor.

"Did you know that the Basque language—Euskara—is totally unique? For example, if you know French, Spanish is pretty easy to learn, because they're related. Or if you know Chinese, you can read some Japanese characters, because they're related, too. But Euskara is one of the only languages in the world that has *no* relatives!"

"It is a strange but beautiful language," the professor replied. "I knew some Basque people in my home country of Peru and tried to learn their tongue. It was quite challenging."

"Their language is a really important part of what it means to be Basque," Elliot went on. "In fact, the Euskara word for a Basque person is *Euskaldun*, which means 'someone who speaks Euskara.'"

"I want to learn their language!" Uchenna replied. "Then I could be an awesome mountain warrior like them."

"I think most of them are shepherds now,"

Elliot said. "Or have normal jobs in cities." But Uchenna had stopped listening. She was banging out a beat on her knees.

"Fearsome warriors in an ancient LAND
Against invaders they would always STAND
What they SPEAK
Is so UNIQUE
Their words are key to their MYSTIQUE!"

"That was inspired by Run-DMC," she informed Elliot and the professor.

"Who?" Professor Fauna said.

Just then, on the edge of the horizon, where the endless blue ocean met the endless blue sky, Uchenna spotted something. A thin strip of green that was growing by the second. "Professor!" she shouted. "I see land!"

Elliot gazed down in disbelief. "I can't believe we made it to Europe."

"And safely, too!" Uchenna added.

Elliot shushed her. "Don't jinx it. We're not on the ground yet."

"Indeed," Professor Fauna agreed. "I usually crash on the *landings*."

They flew over the coast, following a river inland toward the high green mountains. Straddling the river was a city. There were a few tall skyscrapers, but most buildings were fairly low to the ground and had bright red tile roofs.

The riverfront was clogged with factories and warehouses.

"That is the city of Bilbao," Professor Fauna told them. "It is one of the most important cities in the Basque Country. They manufacture many things there. It is where our contact, Mitxel Mendizabal, is from. His family owns one of those factories."

"Is this where we're meeting him?" asked Uchenna.

"No," said the professor. "Mitxel long ago left the family business, and now he lives in the mountains, where he can keep a closer eye on the herensuge."

Fauna guided the plane above smaller villages and valleys, toward a range of tall mountains. The plane headed straight for the tallest of the peaks and then angled toward the flat wooded area below its rocky cliffs.

Gazing out the side window, Elliot said, "Professor, I don't see a runway down there."

"Right. This is why landings are so hard."

Elliot closed his eyes and gripped Jersey to his chest.

"Wait!" Uchenna cried. "There's a field! Land there!"

"Yes! I will try! But as I said, the *Phoenix* usually doesn't *land* so much as *crash*."

Elliot curled up into a ball in his seat. Uchenna noticed that the dials on the dashboard were spinning wildly. "Professor—"

"Not now!" he snapped. The plane was losing altitude quickly. Uchenna's ears felt like someone was shoving cotton into them. "*¡Palabrota!* These controls are useless!" Just then, the plane's nose dipped straight down.

Elliot started to scream. So did Uchenna.

"Hold on!" the professor shouted. "We will crash now!"

CHAPTER NINE

The plane spun as it plummeted toward the earth.

Elliot gripped Jersey with all his might and cursed himself for getting into an airplane with a grown man who believes in unicorns. Without even getting a permission slip from his mom. Of course he was going to die now.

Uchenna was studying the dials and controls, frantically trying to figure out how to pull the plane out of its tailspin.

Professor Fauna was covering his eyes with his arms.

The forest on the side of the mountain was getting very close, very fast. Uchenna yanked on the yoke with all her might. Nothing happened. She smashed some red buttons with her palm. Nothing. She kicked the control panel.

The plane shuddered and stopped spinning. She grabbed the yoke again and pulled back. The plane's nose rose into the air again.

"Hey!" shouted the professor. "What happened?"

"I'm flying the plane!" Uchenna crowed.

Just then, their wings clipped the tops of a clutch of trees, and the whole plane went careening, nose over tail, downward.

Everyone screamed.

"We'redyingwe'redyingwe'redying!" Elliot shouted.

And then, with a horrifying shudder, everything went still.

Elliot, Uchenna, and the professor fell silent. Jersey let out a whine. Smoke rose from the engine. The airplane's propeller was bent like a boomerang.

"Everybody out!" Professor Fauna commanded.

They slid out of their seat belts, opened the plane door, crawled over the white painted metal, and lowered themselves, one by one, to the ground. All three of them were sweating and breathing hard. But they were uninjured. Jersey chirruped in relief.

"I can't believe we're alive," said Elliot.

Uchenna inhaled. The clean mountain air was mixed with the smell of burned engine oil. They were in a grove of tall evergreen trees near the edge of a pasture. Professor Fauna removed a handkerchief from his tweed suit jacket pocket and wiped his brow. "Well," he said, "welcome to the Basque Country!"

POP!

His eyes went wide.

"What was that?" said Elliot.

POP! POP!

"If I am not mistaken—" Professor Fauna said, his head cocked to one side, his eyes wide.

POP! POP! POP!

"Those are gunshots."

POP!

"Hit the deck!" Uchenna cried.

They threw themselves to the ground.

"We'redyingwe'redyingwe'redying!" Elliot whimpered.

"Keep calm!" Professor Fauna said. "I'm sure it's all a misunderstanding!"

POP! POP! POP!

"I understand gunshots pretty well," Elliot replied. "I think they're intended to kill us."

"Or maybe just scare us," Uchenna said. "They don't seem to be hitting anything nearby."

"Can we just tell whoever it is," said Elliot, "that if their intention is to scare us, the gunshots are working, and I am sufficiently terrified?"

"Good idea!" the professor exclaimed. He started to get to his feet.

"What? I was kidding! Don't stand up!" Elliot cried.

But it was too late. The professor was standing. Another shot rang out.

"Hello!" the professor called. "You have succeeded, whoever you are! We are afraid!"

The gunshots stopped.

The children waited, unable to breathe.

There was no sound in the forest but the creaking of the trees.

Elliot braced for another round of gunfire.

Then, a voice called out.

"Defende Fabulosa?"

"Protege Mythica!" Professor Fauna cried. "Mitxel? Is that you?"

A man stepped from the nearby woods. He had a long straight nose, a wispy black mustache, big ears, and he wore a black beret. "Mito!" he cried, throwing up his arms. In one hand, he held a very old-looking rifle. *"Kaixo!* Thank the heavens, it is you!"

"*Kaixo*, Mitxel! It has been too long." (The Basque greeting sounded like *KYE-shoh*.)

The two men embraced.

Uchenna and Elliot stared. Jersey, who was cradled between Elliot's body and the ground, growled menacingly.

But Professor Fauna turned around and said, "Children, may I introduce my dear friend, Mitxel Mendizabal, representative of the Unicorn Rescue Society in the Basque Country!"

Elliot said, "And the man who, just thirty seconds ago, was trying to kill us? How nice to meet you."

"It is nice to meet you, too," replied Mr. Mendizabal. And he sounded like he meant it.

CHAPTER TEN

"I am sorry about the shooting," Mr. Mendizabal said as he led them through the woods, away from the plane. He walked like an aging military commando.

"Oh yeah," Elliot replied. "No problem. Anytime."

"You must be very careful trespassing in the lands of the Euskaldunak. We don't take kindly to it. Just ask the Romans." The grizzled man with the black beret chuckled and hefted his rifle over his shoulder. "But, personally, I have never seen so many trespassers as these days!"

"Trespassers?" the professor asked. "Here?"

"Yes! People are snooping around my property, day and night. Mysterious vehicles drive up the mountain and then, when they catch sight of me, turn around and drive back down. And then my dear herensuge goes missing!" The tough Euskaldun sniffled hard and cleared his throat. Uchenna wondered if he was crying. She'd never seen a man cry while carrying a rifle.

"But what is this?" Mr. Mendizabal suddenly asked, gesturing at Jersey.

The professor told his friend all about Jersey—his flying and his ability to turn invisible in shadows in particular—as they made their way up the mountain. Finally, they came in view of a large farmhouse. "Welcome," said Mr. Mendizabal, "to my *baserri*, my home. It is called *mendizabal*, which means 'house that is close to the wide mountains.'" He gestured at the peaks all around them.

"I thought *your name* was Mendizabal," said Uchenna.

Elliot said, "The Euskaldunak take their names from their family homes. Isn't that right, sir?"

"Indeed it is," agreed Mr. Mendizabal. "This is our ancestral home, and so this is what we are called."

From the outside, Mr. Mendizabal's *baserri* was a strange-looking place, like someone had stapled together a bunch of unrelated buildings from totally different time periods. The ground floor was made entirely of stone, and above it was

another level made from wooden beams joined with plaster. Above that was a high, sloped roof covered in red tiles. There was a rusty yellow pickup truck parked outside.

Mr. Mendizabal led them through the front door into a spare living room, decorated with wood and sheepskins. The air was thick with the scent of baking bread and grilling fish. "Are you hungry?" Mr. Mendizabal asked. "I have made *pintxos!*"

"*PEEN-chohs!* My favorite!" exclaimed the professor.

Mr. Mendizabal led them to a large wooden table in his kitchen and invited them to sit. On the table was a platter of tiny slices of bread, some piled high with bits of sausage, some with grilled fish, and some with roasted peppers. They were held together with toothpicks.

Professor Fauna and Uchenna dug in, making sure to try every kind of *pintxo* on the platter. Jersey liked the fish ones, but didn't bother with the bread part.

Elliot spread a napkin on his lap and eyed the *pintxos* nervously. "What's on these noodles?" he asked as he tentatively helped himself to a bowl of stringy white things flecked with chunks of red and white.

"Ah, that is a local delicacy called *txitxardin*." It sounded like *CHEE-char-deen.* "I cook them in olive oil and garlic, with a bit of hot pepper."

"Mmm!" Elliot said, scooping them into his mouth. "Good!"

"Yes, they are. But they are not noodles. They are baby eels."

Elliot, his mouth full, stopped chewing. His eyes bulged. Uchenna laughed. A moment later, when no one was looking, he managed to take the eels out of his mouth and deposit them in his napkin.

Jersey crawled down into Elliot's lap and ate the half-chewed eels. Elliot tried not to throw up.

CHAPTER ELEVEN

After the *pintxos*, Professor Fauna asked Mr. Mendizabal to tell them of the herensuge.

"Legends of dragons have been told throughout this land. But each region tells its own version of the dragon story. Here in Euskal Herria—the Basque Country—we told stories of a dragon with seven heads: Sugaar, the god of the storms. Nearby, in Cantabaria, they tell the tale of a dragon called the *cuélebre*, who lives in a cave overflowing with treasure. In every town, they tell tales of their own kind of dragon."

Professor Fauna cut in, "It is my belief, children, that all of the dragon legends of this coast are about the *same dragon species*. But each time the story of the dragon is told, it changes. Suddenly, you have ridiculous things like seven-headed dragons, like in a child's game of broken telephoning."

"Wait, you *don't* think there's a seven-headed dragon?" Uchenna asked.

"No, I do not," said Professor Fauna.

"I disagree," Uchenna replied.

The professor laughed. "On what evidence?"

"That seven-headed dragons are awesome, and I want them to be real."

"That is not the basis for a scientific theory, Uchenna."

Mr. Mendizabal shrugged. "I agree with the girl."

"But what about the herensuge?" asked Elliot. "You haven't told us about the one dragon we're here to save."

"Ah!" said Mr. Mendizabal. "I was just getting to her! The legend of the herensuge has been intertwined with the history of my family for generations. It begins more than a thousand years ago, with my ancestor, a sword-smith named Teodosio.

"Tay-oh-DOH-see-oh lived in Bizkaia, the region of the Basque Country where we are right now. He was a true Euskaldun: a proud man, but also a man of honor. He made a guarantee to each person who bought one of his swords that the weapon would never fail in battle. And they never did."

"Wait, does your family *still* make swords?" Uchenna asked.

Mr. Mendizabal frowned. "My brother, Íñigo, runs the family steel foundry in Bilbao, but I do not believe he has many requests for swords these days. His steel is used to build buildings and boats and railroads and other such businessy things."

"Well, if he did have any swords, I might

know someone who would want one," Uchenna said, pointing at herself with both of her thumbs.

"Uchenna," said Professor Fauna, "this is no time for talk of swordplay. That part of your training may come later, but only if you pay attention to these valuable lessons. Please continue, Mitxel."

Instantly, Uchenna sat up as straight as she could, crossed her hands in her lap like a model student, and turned to Mr. Mendizabal. He went on with his story.

"One day," Mr. Mendizabal went on, "a knight's squire burst into Teodosio's workshop. 'Your blade failed,' the squire said, and he tossed a broken sword onto the floor. 'My master was escorting a noblewoman through the mountains. He heard of a dragon living in a cave nearby, so he set out to prove his courage and defeat it. My master fought bravely, but your sword could not pierce the beast's scales. The dragon killed my master and took the lady back to his cave.'"

Professor Fauna threw his arms in the air. "What is this with people attacking dragons all the time? Why can't they just leave them alone?"

"Exactly!" exclaimed Mr. Mendizabal. "Just like the Euskaldunak. We live in the mountains and we just want to be left alone. We need no one!"

Uchenna and Elliot glanced at each other. Who needs *no one*? But they weren't about to question this tough old soldier. He went on:

"Teodosio said, 'I promised that my blades would never fail, and now your master is dead and a noble lady is in danger. Take me to the cave, and I will rescue her!'"

Uchenna raised an eyebrow. "Hold on. Why do the boys have to go and rescue the girl? Why don't they give her a sword so she can rescue herself?"

"This story is very old," said Professor Fauna. "In that time, it was considered wrong for women to fight. I am sure that if you were captured by a dragon, you would not need a boy to save you."

"Especially when I get my own sword."

"You know," Elliot said, "it just occurred to me that we actually *might* be captured by a dragon. Like, in real life. Like, maybe today."

"Don't worry," Mr. Mendizabal assured him. "This herensuge would never capture you."

"Really? Why not?"

"She would just kill you."

All the blood drained from Elliot's face.

Mr. Mendizabal continued with his story. "So Teodosio took the strongest and most perfect blade he had ever made and followed the squire to the cave of the herensuge. There he found the dragon, its scales glistening in the fading daylight, its brown leathery wings outstretched, perched on an enormous pile of treasure. The terrified noblewoman was trapped in the cave behind it.

"Teodosio stepped forward once. He was afraid, but what could he do? He stepped forward again. The dragon watched him come. Teodosio stepped a third time.

"Which is when the dragon lunged.

"Teodosio swung his sword.

"And the greatest blade of the greatest sword-smith in Euskal Herria . . . shattered. It shattered like glass.

"A roar of flame enveloped Teodosio. He fell to the ground, fire covering his body. The floor was damp, though, and there were scattered puddles. Teodosio rolled to a puddle to extinguish the flame. As he did, he felt wings beating the air above him as the dragon flew out of the cave. A moment later, the noblewoman was beside him, bathing his burned skin with water from the puddles. It was blissfully cool. And then, right before their eyes, the burns healed.

"'What water is this?' Teodosio asked.

"'It is the dragon's saliva,' said the noblewoman. 'It is marvelously powerful.'"

"What?!" Elliot exclaimed. "She washed him with *dragon spit*?"

"But of course! Teodosio and the noblewoman

escaped the cave and were mar-
ried. Together they built a
home for their new family.
That home grew and changed
over the years—but still it
stands. In fact, you are sitting
in it right now."

"Whoa," murmured Uchenna. "Is that really
true?"

Mr. Mendizabal smiled and tugged on his
mustache. "My ancestor Teodosio was a real person. He built this house, and his sword-smith
trade grew into a large steel business, which we
still own. For generations, though, my family believed that the story of the herensuge was merely
a fable.

"Until we learned the truth."

CHAPTER TWELVE

"Eighty years ago," said Mr. Mendizabal, "a great villain came to power in Spain. He was called Generalísimo Francisco Franco, and he banned the traditional Basque laws—our *foruak*—and even outlawed our beloved language, Euskara."

"He *outlawed* your *language*?!" Uchenna exclaimed.

"Indeed. We were not even allowed to teach our children what it meant to be Basque. I was born during Franco's rule, so my legal name is

Miguel, because to name a child Mitxel, a Basque name, would have been a crime. You take it for granted that you can speak your language and celebrate your heritage. But for two generations, we were not *allowed* to be Basque. If not for people like my parents, who continued to speak Euskara in secret, it would have vanished forever.

"We Basques, and people all over Spain, fought a war against General Franco and his supporters, the Nazis. My grandfather was in charge of the family steel foundry in Bilbao, where they made military supplies for the Basque troops. One afternoon, my grandfather was driving a truck of these supplies into the mountains when the Nazis began dropping bombs from the sky. The rumble of the explosions rocked the road and shook his truck. They toppled a giant tree, blocking his path.

"He got out of his truck, shook his fist at the Nazi airplanes overhead, and went to push the tree out of the roadway. But as he approached the fallen trunk, it began to stir, and he realized its surface was not covered in bark, but in scales like tiny tortoise shells, shiny and dark, and as thick as a man's thumb. The scaly body rolled over, and my grandfather was face-to-face with the shining yellow eyes and razor-sharp fangs of the herensuge.

"My grandfather recognized the beast immediately as the dragon from our family legend. And he was terrified. The beast pushed herself up. My grandfather stumbled backward. The dragon shook herself, caught sight of my grandfather, and then raised herself to her hind legs. She extended her leathery brown wings, and suddenly she was as tall and broad as the house we are in right now. My grandfather turned to run.

"But just then, another wave of bombs fell.

The ground trembled. The great herensuge fell to the ground. To my grandfather's astonishment, she was whimpering. She was frightened and disoriented by the falling bombs. At that moment, all fear left my grandfather, and he felt only pity for the mighty beast.

"He remembered that the dragon in the legend loved treasure, so he took out his pocket watch—the shiniest thing he owned. He made soothing sounds and waved the watch in front of the dragon. She was mesmerized.

"My grandfather took a step backward, and the herensuge followed, her eyes locked on the glittering watch. He took two more steps, and the dragon stayed right behind him.

"My grandfather got back into his truck and drove away,

dangling the watch out the window the entire time. The herensuge followed my grandfather all the way here, to our ancestral home, then up the mountain to a cave where she could be safe from the war and the falling bombs.

"Since that day, my grandfather kept the dragon safe, and he passed that job down to my father, and my father passed it down to my brother, Íñigo, and me. But Íñigo has never liked taking care of the herensuge. I believe he resents that our father paid so much attention to her. So I look after the herensuge, and he looks after the family business." Mr. Mendizabal scowled. "I must admit, he is very good at running the company. He is always making new deals. Now our family doesn't only make steel, but also laboratory equipment and even medicine. But Íñigo doesn't have much use for things like the dragon that don't earn him a profit.

"So, I have tended the herensuge by myself. I bring her little trinkets from time to time, and ensure the mountain lake near her cave is stocked with fish. I have grown to know her as well as a person can know the herensuge. I know her favorite fish to eat. I know she would rather collect a simple piece of aluminum foil than the most expensive gold coin. I know that she is afraid of thunderstorms and other loud noises. We lived simply, and until this week, that had been enough. She was safe. I was happy. But now she is gone, and I am a failure." Mr. Mendizabal let his head fall into his hands. His shoulders shook with silent sobs.

Uchenna stood up. "When are we going to start *looking* for this dragon?"

Professor Fauna clapped his hands. "You are right! We have spoken long enough! There is a time for learning, and a time for action!"

Uchenna thrust her fist in the air and shouted, "Time for action!"

Mr. Mendizabal sniffed, drew his sleeve across his face, and said. "Yes! Action!"

Elliot raised a finger. "Uh, can I just stay here and continue the learning part?"

CHAPTER THIRTEEN

Mitxel Mendizabal led the group up a steep trail behind his house. Jersey ran out ahead, snuffling up the new smells of the Basque Country. The path zigzagged up the mountain, and soon they were high enough that the sheep in Mr. Mendizabal's field looked like little woolly beetles on a muddy green carpet.

After another half hour of sweaty climbing, the trail opened onto a wide blue lake.

Beyond the lake was a sheer cliff towering hundreds of feet above its shore.

"*Amaaaaazing,*" Uchenna breathed.

"This was worth the hike," Elliot agreed.

They walked around the edge of the lake. Fish nibbled at the surface. With a splash, Jersey plunged into the water and resurfaced with a flopping silver fish in his mouth. He coaxed it down his throat.

As they approached the rock face, the opening of a cave came into view.

Uchenna knelt down. "Look at the size of these tracks!" There were giant dragon footprints crisscrossing the turf.

Elliot felt faint.

"And someone else was here," Uchenna said. "Recently."

Indeed, there were boot prints in a few different sizes and a set of tire tracks. There were also deep claw marks in the turf.

Professor Fauna tugged at his beard and turned to Mitxel, "Is it possible that the herensuge was kidnapped?"

Mr. Mendizabal threw up his hands. "How could someone kidnap her? What power on earth could take a herensuge against her will?"

No one knew. Which made them all rather nervous.

Mr. Mendizabal led them into an immense cave. The daylight streamed in, illuminating tiny trinkets that were scattered all over the damp stone floor.

"She would never leave her treasure like this, all messy and helter-skelter! Always she kept it in a nice neat pile!" Mr. Mendizabal's mustache trembled.

While Professor Fauna comforted his friend, Uchenna and Elliot wandered around, looking for some kind of clue as to who may have taken the dragon.

But as the minutes went by, Elliot became

more and more frustrated. Finally, he threw up his hands. "How are we supposed to find her? What are we even looking for? We're not detectives! And what do we know about rescuing dragons? Also, isn't it time for us to get picked up from school? *Back in New Jersey?*"

Uchenna scowled at the cave, her hands on her hips. "I'll tell you one thing, Elliot. I'm not going to back to New Jersey until we find this dragon."

"Listen to yourself," Elliot pleaded. "We are *in Europe*. Without our parents' permission! Looking for a *dragon*! And you're not going back without *finding* it?"

Uchenna turned her gaze on her friend. "You got that right." Then, she stalked off to the back of the cave. Elliot watched her walk into the darkness.

Uchenna's eyes scoured the ground. At each shiny trinket, she bent over and picked it up. A key chain with multicolored charms. A glittery toothbrush. A piece of construction paper with sparkles glued to it.

Mr. Mendizabal was speaking to the professor. "She lived a very isolated life, Mito. She preferred it. She is like the Euskaldunak that way."

"But the Basque people are not isolated. You trade, you travel all over the world—"

"Bah!" Mr. Mendizabal scoffed. "Maybe Basques like my brother do. But not respectable men like me. If we let this global Mippie Mouse culture invade every corner of our lives, how will we know what it is to be ourselves? Will we even be Basque anymore?"

"Mitxel," the professor replied, "being free

to be yourself is not the same thing as being isolated!"

"Hmph. You sound like my brother."

Uchenna was pushing farther and farther into the darkness. She could barely see the ground. To her left was the great nest of the herensuge—a pile of sparkly objects and hay. It smelled of fish. Ahead of her, the darkness was so thick it looked like a black curtain. Perhaps it was a wall of some kind? She reached out to touch it—and for a moment, she felt like she was flying.

Then, Uchenna realized that she wasn't flying. She was falling.

CHAPTER FOURTEEN

"Uchenna!" Professor Fauna shouted. He had seen her lean forward and then go toppling head-first out of sight. He ran to the edge of the darkness and stopped. Mr. Mendizabal came up behind him. "What is down there?" the professor demanded.

"I don't know! This is her space. I don't violate it!" Mr. Mendizabal replied.

Just then, the beam of a flashlight swept the darkness. Elliot stood beside the two men, raking the light back and forth.

"Where did you get a flashlight?" asked Professor Fauna.

"I found it with the rest of the herensuge's trash," Elliot said.

"Treasure!" Mr. Mendizabal corrected him.

"Do you see Uchenna? *Uchenna?!?*" Elliot's cries echoed in the dark cave.

"You shine the light," Mr. Mendizabal said. "I will climb down after her."

"Mitxel, you can't see a thing!" Professor Fauna objected. "You could fall to your death! Let's get a rope."

"Fall to his death?" Elliot repeated. "UCHENNA!"

Jersey came bounding up to them, stared into the darkness, and began to whine.

"That girl is my guest," Mr.

Mendizabal said. "She is in danger because I failed in my duty to protect the herensuge. I am getting her. Now." And with that, Mr. Mendizabal pulled his beret down tight on his head, tied a piece of rope to a nearby rock, and began descending into the darkness. Elliot shined the light down from above, watching Mr. Mendizabal jam his shoes and fingers into crevices as he lowered himself farther and farther down.

"Can you see her?" Elliot called.

"I believe so! A little farther."

At last, Mr. Mendizabal jumped from the rock face and landed on what sounded, to Elliot, like loose gravel. He could not see, because the beam of his flashlight was blocked by an outcropping of rock.

"I found her!" Mr. Mendizabal called.

"Hooray!" shouted Professor Fauna.

"She is not moving!" called Mr. Mendizabal. "American girl, wake up!"

"Her name is Uchenna!" Elliot cried. He turned on Professor Fauna. "We flew all the way to the Basque Country for him, and he doesn't even bother to learn our names?" Elliot turned back to the darkness. "Oh, Uchenna, what have we done to you!?"

Suddenly, they heard a groan.

"She is not dead!" Mr. Mendizabal cried. "Hooray! She is not dead!"

Elliot leaped into the air and pumped his fist. Professor Fauna let loose a tremendous sigh of relief. Jersey squealed and seemed to accidentally perform a somersault, leaving him lying flat on his back.

"Wake up, American girl!" Mr. Mendizabal said again.

Elliot heard Uchenna say, "Who's there?"

"It is Mitxel Mendizabal, your Basque friend!"

"Dad?"

"Close enough," said the Euskaldun. He lifted Uchenna onto his shoulder and began scaling the rocks.

A few minutes later, Uchenna and Mr. Mendizabal were sitting on the cave floor, Mr. Mendizabal breathing heavily, Uchenna still in a daze. Jersey was licking her face.

Elliot pushed Jersey out of the way and got right in front of Uchenna. "Uchenna! Can you hear me?"

Her eyes looked like she was very far away. "Where am I?"

"You're in a dragon's cave, Uchenna! In the Basque Country!" He looked at the grown-ups. "Yeah, that's not gonna make her any less confused."

Uchenna, her voice sounding very far away, murmured, "Why do you have a flashlight?"

"This flashlight?" Elliot lifted the silver object. "Forget the flashlight, Uchenna, it doesn't matter. You do know that you're Uchenna, right? We *never* should have come here. What were we thinking? Oh, Uchenna!"

Uchenna shook her head, like she was trying to get water out of her ear. "I know who I am, Elliot. Get a grip. I just want to know where you got that flashlight."

"She's okay! She's back!" Elliot cried. "Oh, hooray!"

"Elliot! The flashlight!"

"Forget the flashlight! Uchenna, you're okay!"

"*Elliot!*"

"What? The flashlight? Fine! I found it in the cave. It's one of the dragon's shiny things. Who cares? You're all right!"

Uchenna took the flashlight from Elliot. She turned it over. She pointed to a big *S* in a circle. "I'm asking because that's the logo of Schmoke Industries."

Elliot stared at the flashlight. Professor Fauna and Mr. Mendizabal leaned over.

"*¡Mala palabra!*" the professor cried. "Uchenna, you're right! But . . . it cannot be!"

Elliot muttered, "It is."

Jersey began to whine.

Uchenna looked up at Mr. Mendizabal. "I guess we know who your trespassers are."

CHAPTER FIFTEEN

The sun began to sink behind the mountains as they returned to the *baserri*. Elliot and Uchenna were exhausted and nervous. Of all the people who might have kidnapped the herensuge, why did it have to be the Schmoke brothers? Professor Fauna had been very quiet since the discovery of the Schmoke insignia on the flashlight. He wrung his big hands in his lap. Mitxel was drinking a bitter cider called *sagardoa*, lost in thought.

Jersey had fallen asleep under the table.

"I don't understand," Elliot was saying. "Why would the Schmoke brothers be here?"

"Who knows?" Professor Fauna said, throwing his hands in the air.

"Schmoke," said Mitxel. "I know this name. They are the men whom my brother, Íñigo, partnered with in his latest business deal: SMP—Schmoke-Mendizabal Pharmaceuticals."

"Pharmaceuticals? Like medicine? Okay," said Elliot, "so why would they want to steal a dragon?"

"That's obvious," Uchenna replied. "First, dragons are awesome. Second, if they make medicine, they probably want the dragon's spit. Right?"

"Oh yeah." Elliot nodded. "Good point."

"But, Mr. Mendizabal," said Uchenna, "do you think your brother would help them steal the dragon? Would he sell out your family like that?"

Mr. Mendizabal sighed. "My brother and I do not put our eyeballs together on everything."

"What?" said Elliot.

"I think he means 'see eye to eye,'" said Uchenna.

"Right," said the Euskaldun. "We do not see each other's eyes. He believes in globalization, in the whole world becoming one through trade and money and businesses. To me, this sounds like an Old MacDonald on every corner. Íñigo thinks bringing world culture to Euskal Herria will mean better medicines and technologies. I think it means our children will stop play-ing our traditional games like jai alai and only play YouPads instead. This would be very sad, I think."

"YouPads?"

"Whatever they are called. We fought so bit-terly over this that, in the end, we could agree on nothing. We were forced to divide the family's inheritance. He took the businesses, and he has done very well with them. I care for the herensuge, and I did very well with that, too—until . . ." Mr. Mendizabal's head drooped.

"So, could he have told the Schmoke brothers about the dragon?" Uchenna asked.

"My brother is many things," Mr. Mendizabal said, "but he is not a traitor to the family. To reveal the existence of the herensuge to people as untrustworthy as the Schmoke brothers would be unthinkable."

Professor Fauna suddenly shifted in his chair.

"It would be a treachery beyond belief."

The professor sighed sharply.

"A betrayal more terrible than anything I can imagine."

The professor yanked on his beard so hard some hair came out in his hand. "*¡Palabrota!*" the professor muttered. "Ow."

Elliot turned his attention to Professor Fauna. He was acting even stranger than usual.

Meanwhile, Mr. Mendizabal went on, "We swore an oath of secrecy to our father: that we would never reveal the secret of the herensuge to anyone outside of her circle of protectors. No matter how much money was at stake, Íñigo would not breathe a word of her existence to anyone."

"Well, the Schmoke brothers found out about her *somehow*," said Uchenna.

Suddenly, the professor was shouting. "Why are you looking at *me*?" His eyebrows jagged like thunderbolts.

"I . . . I wasn't . . . ," Uchenna stammered.

"Stop wasting time with these questions!" Professor Fauna barked.

He stood up. Uchenna and Elliot stared, openmouthed. "Mitxel, do you know where the Schmoke brothers' operations are in the Basque Country?"

"Of course! Íñigo and the Schmoke brothers are building a new complex in these very mountains."

"You will take us there!" Professor Fauna said, pointing a finger at Mitxel. "Now!" Without another word, he stormed out of the house.

Elliot and Uchenna watched him go.

"It seems," said Elliot slowly, "that the professor is hiding something."

And Uchenna replied, "Uh, you think?"

CHAPTER SIXTEEN

Mitxel Mendizabal's yellow pickup truck rumbled along the mountain roads. He started by going down into the valley, but when they reached an intersection, he turned the truck right and drove uphill again, past a sign that said: COMING SOON—SCHMOKE-MENDIZABAL PHARMACEUTICALS. BECAUSE YOUR HEALTH IS WORTH *ANY* COST.

Uchenna was hanging out of one window of the truck. Jersey was in his special backpack. Mr.

Mendizabal had stuffed fresh fish in its side pockets, and Jersey was sniffing frantically through the air holes. He seemed to be trying to find a way to open the zipper and get at the fish. Mr. Mendizabal's knuckles were white on the steering wheel as he tried to keep the truck from running off the small mountain roads. Professor Fauna glared out the windshield in silence.

Elliot seemed lost in thought. After a while, he said, "If the Schmoke brothers really have captured the herensuge for its spit, and they want to make a medicine to cure all sorts of diseases, is that really so bad? I mean, they could help a lot of people."

Professor Fauna inhaled and frowned. "Elliot, the oath I swore when I founded the Unicorn Rescue Society was simple. The creatures of myth and legend must be protected. They are few and rare and fragile. Without the society, there would soon be none at all. This herensuge may be the last of her kind. If the Schmokes harm her, no matter how honorable their intentions might be, it could erase a beautiful and noble creature from existence." He sighed loudly. "And I do not believe the Schmoke brothers' intentions are as honorable as you think."

Uchenna gave Elliot a meaningful look. "Professor," she said, "do you want to tell us anything more about the Schmoke brothers?"

Professor Fauna looked out the window and chewed his lip and did not answer. Elliot raised his eyebrows. Uchenna tried again. "Professor Fauna?"

The professor gazed darkly into the early evening.

CHAPTER SEVENTEEN

The truck rumbled up to the laboratory construction site, which was surrounded by a high chain-link fence topped with razor wire. The building was set back from the road, built into a steep rock face. It was still unfinished, but the central wing of the building looked mostly complete, and there were lights on inside.

Mr. Mendizabal pulled the truck into the driveway, bringing them face-to-face with a security gate and a frowning guard. Mr. Mendizabal

quickly reversed the truck around the fence and out of sight. *"Tontolapiko!"* he said angrily. "I apologize," he told the others. "When I was last here, there were no guards."

"There's only one," said Uchenna hopefully. "Maybe we can just run past him."

"What if there are more inside?" asked Elliot. "This one would sound the alarm, and they'd be all over us."

"There is only one option," said Mitxel. "One of us must distract the guard while the rest sneak inside. Since he is my countryman and speaks my language, I am the obvious choice for the diversion. That means, however, I will not be able to accompany you for your assault on the factory."

"Don't worry, Mr. Mendizabal," Uchenna reassured him, patting his shoulder. "We've got this."

"What?" said Elliot. "What do we have? We're supposed to find the dragon without Mr. Mendizabal? And what do you mean *assault*?"

"Don't worry, children," Professor Fauna said.

"I have much experience with mythical creatures."

"With dragons?"

"Well . . . a little."

Elliot buried his head in his hands.

Mr. Mendizabal got out of the truck. "Wait for two minutes, then move quickly. Keep against this fence, close to the ground, and be quiet." He turned to the children. "*Zorte on.* That means 'Good luck.'"

Mr. Mendizabal turned the corner and disappeared behind the fence. Professor Fauna kept time on his watch, which was attached to his wrist by a sparkly pink band and had galloping unicorns on the face. After two nerve-racking minutes, Professor Fauna and the  children crept around the corner after Mr. Mendizabal, staying as close to the fence as they could.

They saw that Mr. Mendizabal was talking to the guard, holding a big map, folding it,

unfolding it, and turning it around in his hands, acting very lost and confused. He and the guard were both looking away from Uchenna, Elliot, and the professor. Mr. Mendizabal asked the guard a question and pointed to his left, but the guard responded and pointed in a totally different direction.

As quickly and quietly as they could, they made it past the guard post, up the driveway, and to the main door of the building. Uchenna tried the door, and it was unlocked.

"This is the second time I've broken into a Schmoke brothers' property this week," Elliot murmured. "I'd never broken into anything before! Ever! What has *happened* to my life?"

"Welcome to the Unicorn Rescue Society," Professor Fauna said. And he led them inside the Schmoke-Mendizabal Pharmaceuticals complex.

They found themselves in a large lobby, still under construction, with exposed girders and electrical wires dangling from the ceiling. On the other side of the lobby was a single cherrywood door. Professor Fauna crossed the lobby and tried the bright brass doorknob. That door, too, was unlocked.

Behind the door was a small room with a few desks, some filing cabinets, and big schematic plans pinned up on the wall.

"A map!" Elliot whispered, pushing past the professor. "Now I feel more comfortable." He craned his neck up to study the plans—they were placed at adult height. Uchenna pulled a chair over, and Elliot gratefully climbed up on it. His thin finger ran over the passageways and schematic lines. "We're here," he announced at last, pointing to a room on the plan. "In the administrative office." He pointed to another area of the plan. "These rooms here are marked research laboratories, these are bathrooms, and this is the cafeteria. These green lines are the motion detectors, these blue ones are the

sprinkler system, these red ones are the com-
puter network cables."

"How do you know all that?" asked Uchenna.

"When I was little, I got separated from my
mom in a big shopping mall. It was the worst
three minutes of my whole life. Now, I try not to
go anyplace where I don't know my way around.

If that meant I had to learn to read forty-seven different kinds of schematic maps, so be it."

"Okay, then, Mr. Map Expert. What's this tangle of blue lines?" Uchenna pointed right in the center of the map.

"That's in the basement. It looks like an intense fire safety system. Sensors and sprinklers and the like."

Uchenna's eyes lit up. "Why would they need an intense fire safety system in the basement, unless—"

Elliot finished her thought. "There was a dragon down there!"

"Brilliant, children!" Professor Fauna said. "Now we can go into the dragon's lair!"

Elliot sighed. "Just another day in the life of Elliot Eisner."

"Yeah," said Uchenna, "because your life is awesome."

CHAPTER EIGHTEEN

Leaving the office, Uchenna, the professor, and Elliot found themselves in a long narrow hallway, with other hallways branching off in various directions. They stopped.

"I think the basement's this way," Uchenna whispered, pointing to her left.

"No," said Elliot. "We need to go right, right, left, downstairs, left, right, then through a big door."

"What? How do you know that?" Uchenna asked.

"It was right there on the plans!"

Uchenna looked at Professor Fauna. The professor just shrugged and followed Elliot to the right.

The twists and turns of the hallway happened just as Elliot said. Right, right, left, then down a staircase. The group's footsteps echoed on the linoleum floors. Elliot wished they could move more quietly. Uchenna peeked around corners and into empty rooms, checking for lurking guards. Professor Fauna was pulling his beard nervously and muttering to himself. Jersey was snoring in his backpack. Elliot couldn't decide who was more useless, Professor Fauna or Jersey.

They reached the basement. Elliot led them left, down a narrow hallway, and then turned right.

At that point, Elliot expected to find the

doorway to a giant room containing the heren-suge, but instead they entered a cozy library, with floor-to-ceiling bookshelves, overstuffed leather chairs, and a fire roaring in the fireplace.

The room was clearly decorated by someone with expensive taste and too much money. On the mantel was a candelabra with seven white candles. On the far wall, a giant painting of an old man glowered at them with cold, glittering eyes. He looked like a king—or at least like he *behaved* like one. He had one hand resting on a globe, while the other held a cigar. The gold nameplate on the ornate frame simply read: SCHMOKE.

The room was deserted, but two tiny glasses on the table—half full of pale yellow liquid—indicated that someone had been there quite recently.

"This can't be right!" whispered Elliot. "The map said this would be a big room with incredibly robust fire safety."

"Are you sure you remembered the right route?" Uchenna wondered. "Maybe it was right, left, right downstairs, right, left? Or right, left, downstairs, left, right, right?"

"Don't be ridiculous," said Elliot. "I can picture the map in my mind. There should be a big door exactly—*HMPH!*"

Just then, Professor Fauna grabbed both children, smothering their mouths with his big hands, and yanked them against a wall. They tried to struggle, but he kept their heads pinned to his chest. Uchenna grabbed his arm and tried to pull it away, but he was too strong. Elliot shimmied to the left and right, but the professor held him tight.

This was it.

They had flown in an airplane with a weird social studies teacher to the Basque Country, without telling their parents, gone with him into the basement of an empty pharmaceutical plant, and now this was the end. Of course it was.

Elliot began to whimper.

"*¡Mala palabra!*" Professor Fauna hissed. "Be quiet, children! And stay still!" He yanked them behind a piece of mahogany furniture and shoved them to the ground.

As they hit the plush carpet, the children saw the fireplace sliding sideways and heard voices echoing . . . from *inside* the fireplace.

CHAPTER NINETEEN

At first, the voices from the fireplace were unintelligible. But as they grew louder, the words became clearer.

"Don't be ridiculous, Milton," one of the voices said. It was gravelly and confident. "These things take time. Íñigo here says this dragon saliva will produce the cure-all, and I believe him."

Three men emerged from behind the fireplace. Two of them wore expensive blue suits, and though one was tall and fit and the other was short and fat, they were, very obviously, brothers. Their eyes glittered like cut gemstones. They had the same thin brown hair on top of high, shining foreheads. They shared the same complacent, I'm-so-rich-I-could-buy-you smile.

They were, of course, the Schmoke brothers.

The third man was a little older, and if you gave him a mustache and a black beret, he would have looked exactly like Mitxel Mendizabal. He wore a suit, too, but even Uchenna and Elliot could tell that it was a lot cheaper than the Schmokes'. He was carrying a clipboard.

The taller Schmoke reached up to the mantel and yanked the candelabra to the right. The fireplace slid slowly back into its natural position.

Professor Fauna's grip on the children relaxed. Uchenna moved her head so she had a better view. Elliot began to pray.

"Mr. Schmoke," said Íñigo Mendizabal to the taller man. "Mr. Schmoke," he said again, looking at the shorter man. "You must understand, these things take time. But with a little more effort, I'm sure we will soon see results."

While Íñigo was talking, the Schmokes walked across the room to retrieve their glasses. They stood in front of the sideboard, only inches from where the children and Professor Fauna were hiding.

"I thought you said you grew up with this thing," Edmund, the shorter Schmoke brother, growled.

The taller Schmoke, Milton, suddenly turned to his brother. In a gentle voice, barely above a whisper, he said, "Edmund, has Íñigo been *lying* to us?"

"No, no, of course not, Mr. Schmoke, and Mr. Schmoke!" stammered Íñigo. "I am . . . confident . . . yes, confident! . . . that within the month my scientists will be able to synthesize the compound for mass production."

"Ha! Mass production?" Edmund Schmoke scoffed. "Who said anything about mass production?"

Íñigo was confused. "Isn't that why we're doing this? So that we can produce a miracle cure in our factory? A medicine like that would help a lot of people. And I'm sure it would be *very* valuable."

Elliot nudged Uchenna.

But Milton Schmoke shook his head like he'd just heard a really bad joke. "Íñigo, my boy. Schmoke Industries already sells plenty of medicine," he said. "We're good at it, and we make a lot of money. Why would we come out with a product that competes with the stuff we already make?" He knocked on the side of his head to show how dumb he thought that idea was. "We're not going to sell this medicine."

"Th-then, what are we doing this for?" Íñigo asked.

"You see," Edmund Schmoke explained, "we

inherited a number of things from our dear old dad. Our dashing good looks, for one. Some money, too, though honestly not all that much by our current standards. And we also inherited an unfortunate case of hereditary baldness."

He pointed a thumb at the portrait on the wall, in which thin wisps of hair were combed from one side of the man's skull to the other. They did a terrible job of hiding that the top of his head was completely bare.

"It hasn't hit us yet, but it's in our genes. We know it's coming, and we're going to be ready."

Uchenna elbowed Elliot. His mouth was hanging open.

Íñigo, too, was shocked. "You went into business with me—and persuaded me to help you get the herensuge—so you wouldn't go *bald*? I trusted you! When you came to me asking about the herensuge, you said no harm would come to her, and we'd make the world a better place."

"And the world will be a better place!" Edmund Schmoke responded. "Can you imagine what a sad, dark place it would be if the world's handsomest billionaires were bald?"

Íñigo appeared speechless.

"Don't forget, we also paid you a *lot* of money to make this happen," growled Milton Schmoke, pointing a thin finger in Íñigo's face. "Once we're done here with the dragon, we'll use this laboratory to make mustache wax, or maybe self-tanning spray, or something else cheap and profitable. And you'll get your fair share. But if you're not happy with this arrangement, I'm sure we can find another business partner who'd *love* to take your seat on the board of directors."

"Milton," said Edmund Schmoke, "I'm sure Íñigo knows how *lucky* he is to have this opportunity."

"Well, my patience is starting to run out," he replied. "If the experiment doesn't yield a positive result in the next forty-eight hours, we may have to renegotiate our deal. You know me, I don't tolerate"—*sniff, sniff*—"do you smell fish?"

Professor Fauna and the children kept perfectly still. None of them made even the faintest sound. Even Jersey's faint breathing inside the backpack stopped. Uchenna inhaled slowly. The smell of fish was definitely wafting from the backpack.

Edmund sniffed the air. "It must be the oysters we ate before our little inspection. That fool butler, Phipps, probably spilled some on our rug."

"It's such a nice rug. And so expensive," Milton observed. "I guess we'll just have to withhold Phipps's pay to cover the cost of replacing it."

"A word of advice, Íñigo," Edmund Schmoke

said, turning to his unhappy business partner. "Good help is hard to find. But even mediocre help is worth holding on to if you can dock their wages so much they have to work for free." He burst out laughing, and his brother joined him.

Chuckling and patting each other on the back, the Schmokes left the library through the non-fireplace door. Íñigo Mendizabal followed obediently behind, head down and shoulders slumped.

CHAPTER TWENTY

When the room was clear, Professor Fauna slowly released the children. They rolled out from underneath the sideboard, stretching their necks and cramped legs. Elliot and Uchenna glanced at the professor. He had scared them, grabbing them like that. But he had been saving them from being spotted by the Schmoke brothers. He had meant well. Maybe he *always* meant well . . . But then what explained his suspicious behavior whenever the Schmokes came up?

"Why are you standing there gaping at me, children?" Professor Fauna demanded. "Let us save the herensuge!" He strode to the fireplace. Uchenna and Elliot shook themselves and followed. Jersey scrabbled at the inside of his backpack, eager to be let out. The professor grabbed the candelabra and pulled it to the left.

The fireplace groaned and lurched open, revealing a dark passageway behind it.

"I *knew* I hadn't misremembered the map," Elliot said. "I just hadn't accounted for a cheesy secret passage!"

"Cheesy?" Uchenna laughed. "There's no such thing as a cheesy secret passage."

"Come on. Fireplace and candelabra? It's the kind of thing I used to imagine when I was like five years ol—"

"Children!" Professor Fauna interrupted. "While I find your argument fascinating, it would be wise to continue on our journey before those horrible men come back."

As they walked through the fireplace, cool, damp air blew past them from deeper in the passage. The only light came from bare bulbs hanging from the ceiling. The walls were rough, and the floor was covered with gravel and the occasional larger rock. It sloped gently downward. The fireplace began to close behind them.

"I think we've left the building and are inside the mountain," Elliot observed. "This was *not* on the map."

"Maybe they've got lots of dragons down here," said Uchenna. "Like the seven-headed one."

"That wasn't a real dragon, Uchenna," the professor reminded her.

"Says you," she replied.

Professor Fauna led the way deeper into the cave, following the shiny pipes and cables attached to the cavern walls. The tunnel took a hairpin turn so they were going back in the direction they'd come—except deeper and deeper into

the earth. Then, the narrow passage opened onto a huge chamber.

The room was bigger than the school cafeteria, and the ceiling was so high that the light from the lightbulbs on the walls didn't illuminate it. The only thing visible above were the tips of pointy stalactites, which glistened as they dripped water to the cave floor.

In the center of the chamber was a small wooden desk covered in papers. On the nearby wall, a number of machines hummed and dials glowed in the darkness. And in the shadows on the far side of the chamber they saw bars. Steel bars.

The steel bars of a massive cage.

Elliot and Uchenna hesitated, staring across the great chamber. Was there a dragon in that cage? A real dragon? Was it possible? From inside the backpack, Jersey started whimpering.

"Okay," murmured Uchenna. "Here we go."

She strode past the desk and into the

shadows. The cage loomed larger and larger and larger. How big could it be? It was nearly as big as Mr. Mendizabal's house. But it appeared to be . . . unoccupied.

"Guys, I don't think there's anything in here."

Jersey was whimpering louder. Elliot and Professor Fauna walked up behind Uchenna. The cage was dark and looming . . . and empty.

"There's no dragon here," said Elliot. "You know, I can't believe I'm saying this, but I'm actually kind of disappointed not to be face-to-face with a dragon right now."

Jersey was scratching uncontrollably at the inside of the backpack. "Okay, okay," Uchenna said. She unzipped the main compartment of it. In a shot, Jersey leaped out and scrambled down to the stone floor.

"Hey! Wait!" Uchenna shouted. But Jersey didn't wait. He went careening around the side of the cage, his wings speeding his little legs along.

Uchenna bolted after him, with Elliot and the professor right behind her.

Jersey ran down the long side of the steel cage until he suddenly came to a claw-and-hoof-scrabbling stop. He stood on the stone floor, his limbs quivering, his little chest heaving. He whined and whimpered and stared at the cage.

"What is it?" Uchenna said. "Jersey, what do you see?"

Elliot grabbed her arm. "*That. That's* what he sees."

Jersey had found the dragon.

CHAPTER TWENTY-ONE

Curled up in the farthest corner of the cage, half shrouded in darkness, was the biggest animal Elliot or Uchenna had ever seen. She—Mr. Mendizabal had called the herensuge *she*—was bigger than the professor's plane, with greenish-brown scales so dark they were almost black and leathery brown wings folded up against her body.

The dragon was chained to the floor with iron shackles, and her head was held in place by a harness above a big stainless-steel vat that was

built into the floor. A nozzle was spraying her face with a fine mist that smelled like a barnyard.

Even though the herensuge couldn't turn her head, she found them with the corner of one of her bright yellow eyes. She began to thrash against her restraints.

"How do we get her out of there?" Uchenna asked.

"Uh, I'm suddenly not sure I want to . . . ," Elliot muttered.

"Elliot!"

"Okay, okay! Then, let's check the desk." He hurried back to the desk and began pushing the papers around. "Maybe there's a key somewhere." But he found no key. "Or maybe they wrote down instructions to open the cage?" There was a notepad with handwritten notes on it. He picked it up and read the most recent note aloud. "'Subject has not yet responded to olfactory stimuli. Must find something more appetizing to promote salivation.'"

"What does that mean?" Uchenna asked.

"They cannot figure out how to make the herensuge drool," Professor Fauna said. "They haven't found a food that's delicious enough."

"I bet *we* could make her drool," Uchenna said. She patted the fish in her backpack.

Jersey was still whining at the dragon.

Elliot picked up other pieces of paper, looking for instructions to open the cage and free the herensuge.

Uchenna searched around the cage. "Hey, there's a door to the cage over here!" Uchenna announced. "And it doesn't have a keyhole. It has a keypad. For a code."

"Show me," Professor Fauna demanded. He strode over to where Uchenna was standing. Elliot gave up on the desk and came over to the door as well. The professor looked at the keypad. His fingers hesitated in the air. Then, he pushed the numbers 3-3-3-3. The lock clicked, and the door swung open.

The herensuge thrashed harder in her restraints.

Elliot and Uchenna stared at the professor.

"How . . . how did you know the Schmoke brothers' passcode?" Elliot stammered.

"They have always used that code," Professor Fauna said, sighing. "It is their father's birthday. March third, 1933."

"And how do you know *that*?" Uchenna demanded.

"Now is not the time—" the professor began.

But Elliot shot back, "I think now *is* the time!" The herensuge thrashed so hard that her steel restraints groaned. "We're about to release a *dragon*, and you've been keeping secrets from us all along! What's your connection with the Schmoke brothers? How do you know so much about them? Mr. Mendizabal's brother said *they* came to him asking about the herensuge. How did they even know about it? *What are you hiding from us, Professor?!*"

Suddenly, the herensuge thrashed, and one of the restraints broke. It sounded like a sheet of metal tearing.

"Elliot!" he barked. "Now is *not* the time. Uchenna, may I have some fish, please? Otherwise, this dragon may be very angry and very hungry and very on the loose."

Uchenna looked between a glowering Elliot and a desperate Professor Fauna. She hesitated.

She handed the professor the backpack. He unzipped one of the side pockets, withdrew a limp silver fish, and strode right up to the struggling herensuge. "Shh," said the professor calmly. "Shhhhh. We are here to rescue you. And we've brought treats."

The combination of the professor's calm voice and the fragrance of the fish seemed to immediately relax the dragon. Professor Fauna waved the fish back and forth and continued to speak to her in a soft, singsongy pattern. *"Yes, herensuge. You're a good herensuge. Such a beautiful herensuge.* Elliot,

Uchenna, while she is looking at the fish, perhaps you can release her restraints?"

Elliot began to protest. "Is that really a good idea? Are you sure?" But Uchenna had already entered the dark cage. She crawled around the herensuge, found the steel pins that held the dragon's shackles in place, and one by

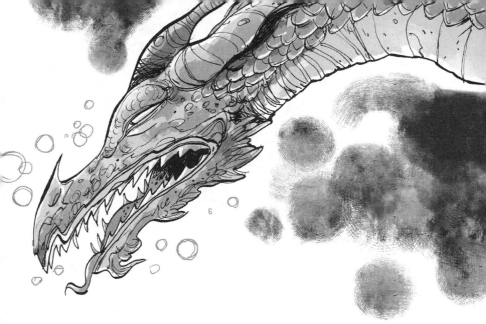

one she removed them. When she had finished, the professor tossed the fish to the herensuge. She opened her mouth to catch it, sending a spray of her saliva into the pan below her head.

As soon as the droplets touched the container's steel surface, the sensors sputtered to life. Lights began to flash and the happy alarm of a successful experiment began to chime up and down the corridor.

"Uh-oh," said the professor.

The herensuge growled.

He threw her another fish.

The alarm continued to sound.

CHAPTER TWENTY-TWO

"Elliot, lead the way!" the professor commanded. He held a fish in front of the herensuge's face. "Uchenna, grab Jersey! I will follow with the dragon!" He continued purring at her. *"Nice herensuge . . . good herensuge . . . pretty herensuge."* He threw another fish to the dragon. She snapped it up in her enormous jaws. Her teeth looked like a hundred bone-white knives.

But as they were leaving the cage, something stopped them dead in their tracks.

"See, Milton?" Edmund Schmoke's voice echoed down the tunnel. "I told you it would work."

The children froze. Professor Fauna froze. The herensuge snapped at the fish in the professor's hand. He released it quickly.

"Professor, throw a fish to the other side of the cage," Uchenna said quietly. "Don't let them see that the dragon's loose. I don't want them to hurt her."

"How could they hurt her?" Elliot whispered. Though they *had* managed to kidnap her somehow. Maybe they had some terrible technology, like an electrode wand or a tranquilizer cannon or a . . . Elliot made himself stop thinking about it.

The professor did as Uchenna suggested. The herensuge lumbered after the fish, back into the shadows. At exactly that moment, the Schmoke brothers emerged into the cavernous laboratory.

Elliot, Uchenna, and Professor Fauna just stood there.

"Milton!" said Edmund, his toad-like face lighting up. "Look who it is!"

"Professor!" Milton exclaimed. "What a lovely surprise!"

Elliot and Uchenna looked at each other. Their stomachs felt empty, hollow.

"Hello, Edmund," said Professor Fauna. "Hello, Milton."

"And you've brought those children who

broke into our greenhouse! All the way to the Basque Country! What trouble you've gone to!"

Professor Fauna tugged on his beard and did not reply.

"You know," said Edmund, "we've never thanked you properly for all this. For teaching us about the herensuge and the Jersey Devil and all the other wonderful mythical creatures of the world."

"Did you know that we're on the verge of curing baldness, thanks to you?" Milton went on. "Not that we need such a cure . . . yet." He adjusted the thinning hair on top of his shiny head. "But where would we be without your tutelage? Your guidance? Your mentorship?"

"Professor," said Uchenna, not taking her eyes off the billionaire brothers, "what are they talking about?"

The Schmokes looked at her and smiled. Edmund said, "He hasn't told you? What good friends we are?"

"We are *not* friends," Professor Fauna said.

But he didn't sound convincing. He sounded miserable.

"Oh, don't be ungenerous, Professor. We were very close friends at one point." Edmund was coming closer to Uchenna and Elliot. Milton was just behind him, his expensive leather shoes crunch-crunching on the stone and gravel floor. Edmund was near enough that the children could smell fancy cologne wafting off his navy-blue suit. "We were very close with the professor for many years, children."

"Yes," said Edmund, waddling into the shadow of his towering brother. "I imagine he's very proud. We haven't forgotten any of the lessons he taught us. We remember everything."

"What are you *talking* about?" Uchenna shouted. Elliot was so afraid his fingers were quivering.

"Are you that stupid, children?" Edmund grinned. "Haven't you figured it out yet? We were just like you, once. The two young assistants in

Professor Fauna's crazy Unicorn Rescue Society. We didn't believe him when he first told us about it, of course. I imagine you didn't, either. He does come off as quite insane, doesn't he?"

Milton laughed. "Oh, he does, he certainly does. However, Professor Fauna is not insane. Foolish, yes. Naïve, absolutely. But not insane. You see, we were students of his at the prestigious Exmoor Boarding School for Young Gentlemen. He taught history and world cultures. We were promising students, I think."

"Oh, very," Edmund agreed. "He began to take us under his wing. To tell us about the creatures of myth and legend. And how he believed that they were real."

"We humored him at first," said Milton, "and laughed behind his back. But when he started showing us *actual* evidence of mythical creatures being real . . . well, that's when things got more interesting."

"We joined his little society," Edmund went

on. "Helped him with it for a while. We even still have the membership cards he made for us." He pulled a small laminated slip from his wallet that said: EDMUND SCHMOKE, JUNIOR MEMBER in metallic ink, next to a drawing of a unicorn. Milton Schmoke displayed his as well.

"But we were just biding our time," Edmund continued. "Waiting for the right moment. And then, that moment came. There was a dragon. Not this one—another one. It laid eggs of pure gold. Professor Fauna feared that its habitat was being destroyed by our father's logging company. He enlisted us to help him save it—"

"But we didn't help him, did we?" Milton cut in. "We made it *look* like we would help him. Instead, we captured the dragon, extracted as much gold from it as we could, and let our father go about his business deforesting the Croatian countryside."

"BETRAYAL!" Professor Fauna suddenly shouted. Elliot and Uchenna jumped a foot. "BE-TRAYAL!" the professor cried again. His fists were shaking, his beard was trembling. He began stalking toward the Schmoke brothers. "I *trusted* you! I taught you everything I knew! To care for these animals! To protect them! To value their lives and their freedom! And you BETRAYED them! Not me! I don't care that you betrayed me! No! It is the *animals* you have betrayed. For that, I will *never* forgive you!"

He was face-to-face with the Schmoke brothers now. He was as tall as Milton, but he looked more physically powerful, and his fury made him terrifying.

The Schmoke brothers tried to edge away from him. "We weren't really looking for your forgiveness, Professor," said Edmund.

"Yes," Milton added, with a bravado belied by his cowering, "we've got too much money to need forgiveness."

"BETRAYAL!" Professor Fauna shouted again. He had nearly backed the brothers up against their machinery. He snatched the laminated cards from their trembling hands as they scrambled to get out of his way. The professor raised the cards over his head and dramatically tore them into tiny pieces. At least, that's what he tried to do. But the laminated plastic wouldn't tear no matter how hard he pulled.

"BETRAYAL!" the professor bellowed. He grabbed a loose rock the size of a grapefruit from the cave floor. He placed the old membership cards on the nearest surface, which happened to be the control panel of the scientific equipment. He raised the rock above his head with both of his hands.

"Professor, don't!" Elliot cried. He didn't know what the machinery did, but he didn't think smashing a rock against it was a great idea.

But the professor's eyes were blazing and his lips were trembling, and he brought the rock down with all his might.

CHAPTER TWENTY-THREE

Professor Fauna's rock smashed into the old membership cards, cracking the plastic laminate and splintering into the machine below them. He raised the rock above his head and slammed it down again. The console crunched under the force of his blow. He brought the rock down again and again, breaking the plastic cards into pieces, not seeming to notice that he was also smashing the buttons and switches. Dials started going crazy, whirring and spinning. Lights flashed.

"Stop!" Edmund Schmoke cried. "Professor, don't do that!"

"Please!" Milton shrieked. "You'll kill us all!"

"LEAVE! THE! ANIMALS! *ALONE!*" Professor Fauna shouted, smashing the machines with the stone.

Elliot and Uchenna gripped each other, and Jersey clung to them both.

A groaning came from the walls of the cavern and then the sound of an explosion, deep in the stone of the cave.

"That's the hydraulic support system, Edmund!" Milton was saying. "The place won't hold!"

"Darn it, I know that, Milton!" Edmund snapped. He dove at the professor and tried to pry him away from the machines, but the professor threw him to the floor. The fat billionaire gazed up at the professor in awe and terror.

The walls of the cavern began to shake.

"Oh no," Uchenna whispered.

A stalactite came crashing down from the

ceiling. In a distant corner, another fell. And another.

Then, they all heard an even more terrifying sound. The roar of a dragon.

The herensuge emerged from her cage. Her wings were spread wide. Her eyes looked wild with fear. She staggered this way and that.

"The dragon's escaped!" Milton Schmoke shrieked. "The dragon's escaped!"

"Oh, save us!" cried Edmund. "Save us!"

The dragon roared and beat her leathery wings as stones came crashing down all around her.

"She's afraid!" Uchenna cried. "Professor, throw her a fish!"

The professor had finally dropped the stone. He stood, staring at the enraged dragon. "What have I done, children?" he said. "What have I done?"

A loud scraping was now coming from behind one of the stone walls. "What is *that*?" Edmund Schmoke wailed.

The backpack, with the dragon's fish, lay on the floor. Elliot dove for it, opened it, and grabbed a handful of fish. He threw them at the dragon. She ignored them.

"That's not good," Elliot murmured.

The scratching behind the cavern wall grew louder. As if the stone was being torn away from within. Then, there was a thunderous crash.

A huge hole opened up in one of the cavern walls.

And standing in that hole was an enormous seven-headed dragon.

CHAPTER TWENTY-FOUR

Professor Fauna, Elliot, Uchenna, and the Schmoke brothers all froze. Their mouths hung open. Their eyes were wider than plates of *pintxos*.

The seven-headed dragon roared. Its central head was the largest, and its roar was the deepest. The six smaller heads all around it writhed and screamed in their own high-pitched bellows of rage.

"Professor," Uchenna said, "I think the storm god Sugaar is real."

"It would appear so," Professor Fauna replied, as if in a trance.

The herensuge beat her wings and roared back at the seven-headed Sugaar. Sugaar stood on his hind legs and blew fire all around the cavern. The humans threw themselves to the ground—the fire rolling inches above their flattened bodies in a great exploding wave.

"Yow!" the Schmoke brothers screamed in unison. They reached up and grabbed their heads. They looked at each other. The hair on the tops of their heads had been singed to a crisp by the dragon's fire. "NO!" they cried.

The herensuge and Sugaar stood, now both on their hind legs, and sized each other up. Sugaar blew flames into the air. The herensuge did the same.

The humans gaped in awe and terror.

And then, battle was joined.

Sugaar leaped at the herensuge. The herensuge rose and met him in the air. They tussled, the seven heads of Sugaar biting the herensuge's neck and head and wings.

"They're going to kill each other!" Uchenna cried.

"They're going to kill us, too!" Elliot added.

"Now's our chance!" hissed Milton. "Edmund, come on! Let's go!"

The Schmoke brothers began crawling on their bellies toward the dark corridor that led back to the library, their scorched heads blackened and hairless. "Let's get the

guards!" Edmund was saying to Milton. "And send them back for *all* the dragons!"

"Come, children," said the professor. "We must go, too. And quickly!" He got on his knees and pulled them after him, away from the battle of the dragons.

Fire was exploding from eight mouths. Wings were beating. Elliot and Uchenna followed the professor without taking their eyes off the dragon battle. Then, Uchenna exclaimed, "Oh! One of the heads came off!"

Professor Fauna turned to look.

It was true. One of Sugaar's heads had become detached and now seemed to be crawling, of its own accord, down the herensuge's back.

"What the . . . ?" Elliot whispered.

The herensuge and Sugaar continued wrestling, pushing each other back and forth, toward the cage and then away from it.

Another head came off Sugaar. And another. They flapped around on their own.

"What is going *on*?" Elliot marveled.

Uchenna said, "The dragons don't really seem to be hurting each other. The heads just keep coming off and flying around."

Indeed, as the members of the Unicorn Rescue Society watched, something amazing dawned on them.

"They're not fighting," said Elliot. "They're playing."

"And that's not Sugaar," said Professor Fauna. "That looks like a male herensuge. And those six little heads aren't heads. Those are *baby dragons*."

"I think," said Uchenna, "that we're watching a family reunion."

Elliot, Uchenna, and Professor Fauna watched as the herensuge family played and cuddled and roughhoused together.

Suddenly, Elliot said, "Where's Jersey?"

Uchenna pointed. "There!" Jersey had crawled over to the herensuge family and started growling at one of the babies. The baby, which was much, *much* larger than Jersey, growled back. The two danced around each other for a second and then began tussling on the ground. They were of such different sizes that it looked like a kitten wrestling with a dinosaur.

Elliot rubbed his head in disbelief.

CHAPTER TWENTY-FIVE

Suddenly, a huge stone crashed to the ground, right beside the three members of the Unicorn Rescue Society.

"We must leave this cave," said Professor Fauna. "Now."

"But we can't leave the herensuge family!" objected Elliot. "We've got to get them back to Mitxel! What if the Schmokes come back with guards and guns? Or the cave crushes the whole dragon family? Then, all of this would have been for naught!"

"I don't know what 'for naught' means, but I agree," said Uchenna. "We should lead them out of here!"

"But how?" Professor Fauna had picked up Jersey's backpack and extracted another fish. "There are very few left! Not nearly enough for an entire family of herensuge."

Elliot grabbed the fish. "We don't need the entire family to follow us! We just need to lure *one*! One of the babies!" He ran toward Jersey, who was still tussling with the young herensuge. For one instant, Elliot thought, *I am running toward*

eight dragons who are wrestling and blowing fire at one another. And then he decided to stop thinking, because he was pretty sure that if he thought about it too much, he would faint. Instead, he said, "Here, Jersey! Here, boy!"

Jersey looked up. The horse-size baby dragon that Jersey was playing with cuffed the little Jersey Devil so hard he went rolling across the ground. But Jersey stood up on his four little legs, unfazed, and click-clacked over to the fish Elliot held out. The baby herensuge saw where Jersey was going and began to follow the fish, too. Elliot started to walk backward, leading the baby dragon and the Jersey Devil, toward the tunnel that led up to the library.

"Not that way!" Uchenna said. "We can't lead the dragons right back to the Schmokes and their guards. Follow me!" She made her way toward the hole in the cavern wall that the herensuge family had made. "There must be a whole network of caves down here," she said. "Maybe there's a way out." She and the professor led the way, and Elliot followed behind, holding up the fish. Jersey and the baby herensuge followed Elliot. Soon the entire herensuge family had fallen in line. It was as if, now that they were together, they didn't want to be separated again.

"This is the craziest thing I have ever seen," Elliot murmured.

Uchenna led them deeper and deeper, following the twisting path of the ancient cave. The atmosphere became gloomier and thicker. Their footsteps barely echoed now in the darkness. Sometimes a baby dragon got too close to Elliot, and he tossed them the fish in his hand.

"We better find a way out of here soon," Elliot said. "I'm running out of fish."

"If we go very much deeper, children," said Professor Fauna, "I fear we will run out of air."

Jersey watched another fish sail over his head and into the mouth of a baby dragon. He whined. Then, his whine became more energetic, more curious. Suddenly, he scurried ahead of Uchenna and then up a steep incline.

There was a crack in the cave wall, not quite as big as the little Jersey Devil, and the last rays of sunset were filtering in from the other side.

"Good job, Jersey!" said Uchenna. "I don't think we can fit through there, but that's a good sign. Keep looking for openings, little guy!"

"The sooner the better," said Elliot. "If I run out of fish and these herensuge are still hungry, they might try to eat something—or someone—else." He tossed a fish into the daddy herensuge's mouth, then reached into his bag for another. He groped around for a moment before turning the bag upside down. It was empty.

Uchenna looked at Elliot, holding the empty bag. She looked at the eight dragons, shuffling down the dark cave after her, their leathery wings beating with each step, their tiny dragon eyes glowing. She looked up at the crack in the cave wall.

"Professor," she said, "you have a watch, right?"

"Of course!" he said. He held up his wrist, showing off his unicorn watch with the sparkly band.

"Give it to me," she said.

"No! I won this watch in a very difficult game in an arcade!"

Uchenna raised an eyebrow.

"Of course. Sorry. Here it is." The professor

took off the watch and handed it to her. Uchenna started waving the watch back and forth in front of a baby herensuge's face. The glitter on the watchband caught a beam of sunlight. The herensuge was enchanted. It forgot all about fish.

Eyes fixed on the glitter, the baby dragon took a shuffling step toward Uchenna. Then another. Uchenna took a step backward, only to find herself up against the cave wall.

Before the baby dragon could take another step, Uchenna drew the watch back behind her head and extended her other arm like she was about to throw a football, and then hurled the watch at the hole in the wall. It clattered through, disappearing into the evening.

"Whoa!" said Elliot. "What a throw!"

The baby dragon went bounding up the incline after the watch. It scrabbled at the opening, trying to get through.

"Come on," Uchenna murmured. "You can do it."

The baby dragon tried to scrape the rocks away, but she made very little progress. Uchenna turned away, her shoulders folding in on themselves. "That was my best idea," she said. "Now we'll never—"

BOOM!

The mother herensuge—Mr. Mendizabal's herensuge—crashed through the tiny stone crack after the watch. Suddenly, there was a giant hole in the stone wall. The dragons all clambered up after the mother and went flapping up into the beautiful Basque mountain evening. Even in the distance, they could see Professor Fauna's watch sparkling as it dangled from the mother herensuge's talon.

Professor Fauna, Elliot, and Uchenna climbed up the stone face into the dying daylight. They turned their heads upward, watching the dragons gain altitude and make the formation of a V, like geese flying home after a long winter. The dragon family was heading in the direction of Mr. Mendizabal's house.

Jersey climbed up on Uchenna's shoulders. Elliot beamed at her. "That," he said, "was awesome."

Uchenna smiled. "Let me know if you ever want lessons on throwing like a girl."

"Uchenna," said the professor. "I am very impressed. But," he added, "I really did like that watch."

CHAPTER TWENTY-SIX

When Uchenna, Elliot, and Professor Fauna finally climbed the hill leading to Mr. Mendizabal's house, he was waiting for them in the driveway, covered in grease and motor oil. The *Phoenix*, Professor Fauna's plane, stood beside him. It looked even more dented and scratched than it had before, but the propeller was twirling slowly, as if cooling down from a successful test run.

"We did it, Mr. Mendizabal!" Uchenna shouted.

"It is such a relief," he replied, his smile so broad that his mustache bristled like a toothbrush. "I saw her return to her cave just a few moments ago. And with her whole family! Never did I know she had a mate! And babies! So many wonderful babies!"

He beckoned them inside. But on the threshold, they stopped.

Íñigo Mendizabal stood in the center of the front room, his suit stained with sweat.

Uchenna demanded, "What's he doing here?"

Mr. Mendizabal walked in and put his hands on his hips. Everyone was gazing at Íñigo.

Mr. Mendizabal spoke to the children and Professor Fauna without taking his eyes off his brother. "Íñigo just told me that he helped the Schmoke brothers kidnap the herensuge."

"Treachery!" Professor Fauna cried.

Íñigo Mendizabal bowed his head. "It is true. And I have begged my brother for forgiveness. I thought I was sharing with the world the glory of Euskal Herria! The power of our dragon, helping and healing the whole globe!"

"She is not *our* dragon," his brother chided him. "She is her own."

Íñigo nodded and sighed. "That is true. I was wrong. But no mistake was more grave than trusting the Schmoke brothers. I was a fool."

Mitxel Mendizabal turned to Professor Fauna and the children. "After leaving you at the factory, I returned to fix your airplane—I thought you might need it to escape the Schmokes. As I was finishing the job, Íñigo came running up the mountain, begging me to help him rescue the herensuge. He had no idea you were already in the process of freeing her!" Mitxel laughed, grabbed his brother around the neck, and rubbed his head. "*That* is the way of the Mendizabal family! He was ready to fight the treacherous villains! When we saw the dragon family flying back to

their cave, we leaped in the air and danced with joy!"

Uchenna looked up the mountain toward the herensuge's cave. "What if the Schmokes come back? They know where to find her now."

"That is an excellent question," Mitxel Mendizabal replied. "Luckily, it is a question I have been prepared to answer ever since I began to care for the herensuge. These mountains are full of uncharted caves. Seriously, it is like Swiss cheese in there. I already know of two others, both far from here, that would make ideal lairs for the herensuge. She and her family would be safe, and the Schmokes would not know where to find her."

"May I ask a scientific question?" Professor Fauna said. "Will she really live with her family? I thought the herensuge, like the Basque people, wanted to be left alone."

"Ah no!" Íñigo Mendizabal exclaimed. "*This* is what my brother never understood!"

"I understand everything!" objected Mitxel.

Íñigo laughed. "No, you don't. Independence, yes! But isolation, no! They are not the same thing! We can live by our own laws—relying on the strength of our own hands—but we can also reach out our hands to the rest of the world. One Euskaldun is strong. But with the strength of our families and neighbors, we will endure forever."

Mitxel Mendizabal gazed at his brother. "Maybe today, brother, I understand what you mean. For the first time."

"And I understand that our heritage is too precious to ignore," said Íñigo. "I shall help you protect this beautiful family of herensuge. And the Mendizabal family, too." He reached out his hand to his brother. Mitxel grabbed it and pulled him in for a hug.

Professor Fauna turned to the two children.

"I am sorry that I did not tell you of my history with the Schmoke brothers. I have been ashamed of my failure with them. That is why, for so many years, I have worked alone. But today, I witnessed firsthand what can be accomplished with courage, teamwork, and courage!"

"You said courage twice," Uchenna pointed out.

"I know. And I know that together we are capable of great things, children. It will be very difficult and take much planning and training, but I believe that someday we will be able to undo all of the damage the Schmoke brothers have done to the world and its creatures.

"For this reason, I will do what I have not done in many, many years. Not even the Schmokes were given this honor when they were my students."

The professor reached into his pocket and pulled out two silver rings. They were thick, with flat tops engraved with the silhouette of a unicorn. "Uchenna. Elliot. Please take these rings and wear them as a symbol of our fight against all those who would harm the precious creatures of myth and legend. You are now true and full members of the Unicorn Rescue Society."

"Coooool," Uchenna said, trying the ring on her pinkie, then her index finger, then her thumb. Elliot held his up to the light to inspect the delicate engraving of the unicorn.

"Wear them proudly, but keep them safe," Professor Fauna went on. "For we will use them to identify ourselves to other agents around the world. Inscribed within is our secret motto: *Protege Mythica. Defende Fabulosa.* 'Protect the mythical. Defend the imaginary.'"

Uchenna and Elliot practiced saying the words: "*PROH-te-geh MIH-tih-kah. Day-FEHN-deh Fah-boo-LOH-sah.*"

"Now," the professor said, "we must return to New Jersey. We will meet again tomorrow after school, in my office, where I will teach you more of the secrets of our society."

"Good-bye, children," Íñigo Mendizabal said. "Thank you for what you did."

Mitxel Mendizabal raised his hand in a salute. "It has been an honor to work with you. *Protege Mythica!*"

"*Defende Fabulosa*," replied Elliot and Uchenna.

Jersey stuck his head out of his backpack and chirped. It sounded a little bit like "*Defende Fabulosa*." Or maybe, "I'm hungry. I'm hungry."

It was hard to tell.

CHAPTER TWENTY-SEVEN

As Elliot walked through the front door of his house, his mother called from the kitchen. "Honey! What kept you so long?"

Elliot looked up at the clock on the wall. Five thirty. He entered the kitchen, which smelled of roast chicken, celery, and carrots.

"I got a call from your teacher, Mr. Fauna, saying you were joining a club of his? I thought you were joining the band!"

"It's *Professor* Fauna, Mom."

"Oh, he's a professor? Well, this Worm-Nutrition Club sounds very . . . um, interesting."

"Uh, yeah. It is. I guess."

"Okay. Well, I suppose I don't mind you coming home a little late from school. As long as you're doing something educational. Have you made any friends yet?"

Elliot thought of Uchenna and Jersey and Professor Fauna, of Mitxel and Íñigo Mendizabal, and even of the family of dragons. In his pocket, he felt the cool metal circle of his signet ring.

"Yeah," he said at last, "I've made a few."

In her house, one block away, Uchenna sat down with her father in front of a plate of grilled fish and sautéed spinach. Her mother was working late again. As Uchenna shook hot sauce onto the fish, her dad studied her.

"Sweetie, did something happen to your head today?" Mr. Devereaux asked.

Uchenna reached up and touched her hairline on the right side of her head. A bump had formed from her fall in the cave. "Yeah, Dad, but it's no big deal."

"Did it happen when you were in that club you've joined? With Professor Fowler?"

"It's Professor *Fauna*. Yeah, Dad. But it's fine."

Mr. Devereaux watched her for a moment in silence. Uchenna kept her eyes firmly on her food. She didn't think she could explain everything that had happened that day. Finally, Mr. Devereaux went back to eating. Uchenna was about to exhale when he said, "I just don't want you getting into any trouble."

"Trouble?" Uchenna said nonchalantly. Under the table, she ran her thumb around the edge of her new ring. "Come on, Dad. It's a club at school. You think they'd let us do anything *dangerous*?"

He looked up again and raised an eyebrow.

"Well, we don't. It's a totally normal club."

"Mm-hmm," said Mr. Devereaux, going back to his food.

Uchenna said it again, "Totally, totally normal."

In a dark hallway of South Pines Elementary School, Professor Fauna walked with a hunch, his eyes wild and wide-open, listening intently.

"Heeeeere, Jersey," he murmured. "Heeeeere, little Jersey . . ."

The sound of scrabbling to his left made him jump. He ran after it, into a kindergarten classroom.

Had anyone else been in the school, they would have heard the professor's voice echoing down the halls.

"Not the fish tank, Jersey! Stop! Stop! Those are the kindergarteners' fishes! *JERSEY!*"

ACKNOWLEDGMENTS

JUST AS IT REQUIRES A NETWORK OF PEOPLE AROUND the world to protect the creatures of myth and legend, so does it require a network of people around the world to create the Unicorn Rescue Society series, and this book in particular. We'd like to thank everyone who helped us share the amazing exploits of the Unicorn Rescue Society, but particularly we'd like to thank:

Nikki Gorrell, assistant professor of anthropology at the College of Western Idaho and expert on the Basque Country and Basque mythology in particular.

Izaskun Kortazar Errekatxo, a proud ambassador of Basque culture and language (and pronunciation!).

Jesse's friendly hosts in Euskadi: Maria Carmona Castellano at Urresti, Maria Luisa Urrestarazu at Oiharte, and Stephanie Oxarango at Ondicola.

Emma Otheguy, who, in addition to being an author of an upcoming URS book, also happens to be a scholar of Basque history in the Americas.

Anne Heausler, copy editor extraordinaire.

Xamar, for creating an unbelievable resource in *Orhipean: The Country of Basque*. A book every kid who's curious about the Basque Country should own!

And, finally, to Ricardo Yanci and the children of St. Joseph's School in Boise, Idaho, for your very honest, and very helpful, opinions about this book—from the representation of Basque culture to your demands for pictures. (So, what do you think?)

Adam Gidwitz taught big kids and not-so-big kids in Brooklyn for eight years. Now he spends most of his time chronicling the adventures of the Unicorn Rescue Society. He is also the author of the Newbery Honor–winning *The Inquisitor's Tale,* as well as the bestselling *A Tale Dark and Grimm* and its companions.

Jesse Casey and **Chris Lenox Smith** are filmmakers. They founded Mixtape Club, an award-winning production company in New York City, where they make videos and animations for all sorts of people.

Adam and Jesse met when they were eleven years old. They have done many things together, like building a car powered only by a mousetrap and inventing two board games. Jesse and Chris met when they were eighteen years old. They have done many things together, too, like making music videos for rock bands and an animation for the largest digital billboard ever. But Adam and Jesse and Chris wanted to do something *together*. First, they made trailers for Adam's books. Then, they made a short film together. And now, they are sharing with the world the courage, curiosity, kindness, and courage of the members of the Unicorn Rescue Society!

Hatem Aly is an Egyptian-born illustrator whose work has been featured in multiple publications worldwide. He currently lives in New Brunswick, Canada, with his wife, son, and more pets than people. Find him online at metahatem.com or @metahatem.

PHOTO CREDIT: Michelle Pinet